The Lost Ryū

The Lost Ryū

by

Emi Watanabe Cohen

LQ

LEVINE QUERIDO

Montclair | Amsterdam | Hoboken

For Risa and Seiji, with all my love.

This is an Arthur A. Levine book
Published by Levine Querido

LQ
LEVINE QUERIDO

www.levinequerido.com • info@levinequerido.com
Levine Querido is distributed by Chronicle Books, LLC
Text copyright © 2022 by Emi Watanabe Cohen

Library of Congress Control Number: 2021943720
ISBN: 978-1-64614-132-6
Printed and bound in China

MIX
Paper from
responsible sources
FSC
www.fsc.org
FSC™ C144853

Published June 2022
First Printing

I

Anger and Memories

There were no big dragons in Japan, and there hadn't been for a very long time. To most kids Kohei's age, full-sized ryū felt about as real as the cowboys in American films— maybe they had been a part of history once, but now they were the stuff of legend. Nobody expected to run into John Wayne on their way to the market, and no one had encountered a big ryū since bombs fell over Hiroshima and Nagasaki almost twenty years ago.

Kohei was ten years old. He shouldn't have been able to remember the big ryū at all. He shouldn't have known how enormous they were, or how their tails could crush entire apartment buildings with a single careless swipe, or how their bodies coiled as they lumbered through the cracked streets, slow and majestic, thick tufts of fur glimmering in

the wind. He *definitely* shouldn't have remembered the sound of their talons crunching against asphalt.

But as most kids know, *should* has very little to do with memories.

Kohei remembered the ryū parade.

It couldn't have been a dream—it was so real, so much like a memory. It *had* to have happened in real life. The streets were well-weathered and worn, and the skies were clear and bright, and when Kohei tilted his head back, he spotted a Western dragon circling high in the clouds. It had such huge, pointy wings—Western dragons looked more like birds or bats than the serpent-like Japanese ryū that Kohei was accustomed to. He had never seen a real Western dragon before, and he thought this one was unspeakably beautiful, in a brutal sort of way.

Kohei wanted to be beautiful and brutal. And he *so* wanted to fly. Japanese dragons—ryū—could technically travel through the air, but only when it was raining. They were creatures of water and mist. The ancient ryū that lived thousands of years ago had harnessed the clouds in order to fly, shaping the air with their talons; unless it was raining *really* hard, the tiny ryū that lived in Japan now could barely even hover.

In Kohei's impossible memory, the crowds of people jostling around him barely seemed to notice the circling Western dragon. They were too busy staring at the parade of ryū marching down the street. Kohei didn't mind the jostling, for the most part, and he didn't bother looking at the people's faces. Except one.

His grandfather's.

Ojiisan stood near the front of the crowd, gazing at the big ryū with an odd look in his eyes. He was younger, much younger than Kohei had ever seen him—he had dark hair and brush-thick eyebrows, and his familiar face seemed fuller than usual, even though he'd clearly been starving for months.

His eyes were different too. They were clear, shrewd, and focused. The grandfather Kohei knew was loud and bitter and numb, and he drank too much to focus on anything. And without a little ryū on his shoulder, he was always alone. Lots of people outlived their ryū, but most found new ones to keep them company after a while— Ojiisan never had, and now he was too tired to even try.

This was the only memory Kohei had of the big ryū, and it wasn't even a memory he was supposed to have. He had to assume that made it important. So when Ojiisan had too much to drink and started throwing things against the wall, Kohei went over that impossible memory in his mind, over and over again, studying every detail. Trying to figure it out.

Twenty years ago, Ojiisan had tears in his eyes— maybe tears of joy, maybe tears of sorrow. *Real* tears, either

way. And he was looking up at the big ryū as they marched through the street. There were no big ryū left in Japan anymore, and Ojiisan never laughed or cried. He only yelled and drank.

Therefore, Ojiisan missed the big ryū.

It was the simplest conclusion Kohei could come to. His father would have called it "Occam's Razor," which meant: *the most straightforward answer is the one that's most likely to be true.* If the big ryū came back, Ojiisan would finally be able to feel good things again. He *needed* them to come back.

Which was unfortunate, because big ryū were even less real than cowboys. At least John Wayne was still alive—the big ryū were extinct, and had been for nearly twenty years.

Kohei shuffled into his room and flopped down across his mattress. His own little ryū, Yuharu, clambered from the dresser to the bedpost and settled by his ear. She was small and pink, with cream-colored spines, long whiskers, and a talent for sarcasm. "Tired?" she asked.

"Not really," Kohei said. "But Ojiisan is angry again."

"Oh, what a *surprise.*"

Kohei ignored her. "It's because he's getting older, I think," he said. "Old people are always grumpy."

"You get older every day, and you've never thrown plates against the wall."

"He didn't throw *plates*."

Yuharu prodded Kohei's cheek with her talon until he looked at her. She raised one tufty, skeptical eyebrow.

Kohei groaned. "He didn't!" he exclaimed, shrugging her off. "It was just empty bottles. We don't need those for anything."

Yuharu pulled a cherry blossom from the pouch around her neck and contemplated it, flicking it between her claws like a playing card. "You don't have to defend him, you know," she said. "*I* think your mother should've sent him away years ago."

"She can't do that—he's her father!"

"He's not good for you. All you ever think about is how to make him happy."

"She's supposed to respect him."

"But she's supposed to take care of *you*." Yuharu poked Kohei's cheek again, more gently this time. "She's supposed to be your mother."

"She *is* my mother. And Ojiisan is my grandfather. End of story."

Yuharu studied his face. "Ryū respect our elders," she said, "but we don't often love them. That's why we love our humans so much—because they know how to love us back."

Kohei scowled. He'd enjoyed Yuharu's profound riddle-speak when he was little and still believed in mysterious things, but now that he was ten he preferred a straight answer every once in a while.

He leaned back against his pillows, gazing up at the long, thin crack in his bedroom ceiling. It reminded him of the eastern coast of Japan—curved like a crescent moon but not nearly as smooth. Mama always said she'd patch it someday, but she'd never gotten around to it.

"Yuharu?" Kohei said.

"Eh?"

"You're wrong about my grandfather."

"Kohei-ya . . ." Yuharu flopped onto Kohei's pillow in exasperation.

"It's true! There are times when he's kind. Do you remember when I fell down the stairs last year?" Kohei rolled onto his shoulder. "Ojiisan was the one who found me—he picked me up, and he *hugged* me." It had been the best hug in the world, tight and real. "He didn't say anything, but he was worried. He really cared."

"Mm-hm," Yuharu murmured. She wasn't convinced—she never was.

Kohei plucked her from his pillow and set her back on the bedpost. "It doesn't matter," he said firmly. "Ojiisan is a good person—he just needs something to remind him how to feel happiness. Someday, I'll find a big dragon for him, and then he won't feel so alone, and he'll be happy again. And Mama will stop worrying, and we'll be a real family. Okay?"

Yuharu was silent.

"When I'm older," Kohei promised. "When I'm older and braver and stronger, I'll go on a quest to find a dragon, and everything will be better."

"Of course," said Yuharu.

"Ojiisan will be happy."

"Yeah."

"And you'll be there to help me?"

Yuharu huffed indignantly. "I'd be there if you told me you wanted to eat the *moon*," she said.

That time, Kohei knew she meant it.

2
Last-Minute Cartography

*M*ama's *ryū, Hana, was a* practical sort of creature; she wasn't as talkative as Yuharu, but she had very sturdy teeth. Kohei shuffled into the kitchen the next morning to find her on the floor, selecting her breakfast from the neat heap of glass shards Mama had swept up the previous night. Mama was heating water for tea. She turned to smile at Kohei when she heard his footsteps.

"Good morning!" she said, a little too brightly.

"Good morning," Kohei echoed. He settled in his usual seat. "Is Ojiisan okay?"

Mama forced a smile. "Daijōbu," she said.

That was Mama's favorite word—another way of sweeping up glass shards. "Daijōbu" meant *it's okay*, and it was almost always a lie. Kohei bit his tongue.

The ryū settled into their usual spots on the kitchen counter. Yuharu clambered up the length of the faucet and perched there, keeping a watchful eye on Kohei and his mother, while Hana piled her glass shards next to the sink. Hana didn't like high places—her ancestors had lived with Mama's family near Ōsaka, which was low and humid and never very cold. But Yuharu's ancestors were Hokkaidō ryū, from Papa's side of the family, so she liked snowy mountain mornings and being high up. Kohei liked those things too. It made him wonder what likes and dislikes Ojiisan had shared with his own ryū, back when he'd actually had one.

Kohei kept his eyes on his breakfast, which looked less appetizing than usual. "Mama," he said, "is my grandfather going to be okay?"

"Of course," Mama said, like it was obvious. "He's always okay. He just spends too much time wishing for things he can't have, that's all."

Always okay. Did she really expect him to believe that? Kohei pressed his eyes shut until he saw red, then jabbed at his breakfast until his nattō looked like rubber cement.

There was a phrase that explained why Mama didn't like talking about unpleasant things. Kohei's teachers and classmates said it all the time: "shikata ga nai." It meant *there's nothing to be done*—move on, carry on, and don't brood over things that can't be helped.

When Kohei was little, his father always told him to ignore anyone who said that. "You don't say, 'shikata ga nai,'" he'd whisper. "You say, 'yamenaide, yamenaide.' *Do not quit.* You must keep trying to make things better, Kohei, because there are *always* good things you can do."

Most of the time, Kohei couldn't remember what Papa's voice sounded like—he hadn't heard it since he was three, and three-year-olds don't pay enough attention to silly, important things like voices. But whenever Kohei thought those words—*don't quit, don't quit*—they were always in his father's voice.

Arahata Denjirō's voice was mittens on a cold day. A lullaby. Soft and slow and sure. *Yamenaide, Kohei-kun. Don't quit. There are always good things you can do.*

But Papa wasn't here anymore, so Mama's voice was always a bit louder. *It's fine, Kohei, daijōbu.*

Don't quit!

It's fine.

Don't quit!

It's fine.

Don't quit!

Kohei shoveled the rest of his breakfast into his mouth and forced himself to swallow.

Ojiisan slept straight through breakfast that day. Even Mama started to look a little annoyed with him. "Today of all days," Kohei heard her mutter as she tied her apron strings and headed for the door. "Not that he would've been much help, but still . . ."

"What's wrong with today?" Kohei asked. He gathered up his dishes, then went to retreive Yuharu from the faucet. She didn't enjoy being left out of important conversations any more than he did.

Mama glanced back at him. "It's Sunday," she said, plucking the feather duster from its spot behind the piano.

"Right," said Kohei. "Are Sundays important?"

Yuharu dug her talons into his shoulder. "Sunday," she said through gritted teeth. "It's *Sunday.*"

"Yeah. It comes after Saturday but before Monday. It—oh!" Kohei jerked upright, and Yuharu had to grab his ear for balance. "*This* Sunday?"

Mama's lips pressed into a hard line. "You need to learn to keep track of time," she reminded him.

"I know, I know. Gomen!" Kohei's heart was pounding as if he'd run a mile—he *had* lost track of time. Ojiisan owned their whole two-story apartment building, but since their small family only needed one floor, Mama sometimes found tenants for the smaller downstairs unit. The last renters had mostly kept to themselves—they were an older couple who had cats instead of kids. But Mama

had said this new family would be different somehow . . . what was it she wanted Kohei to do for them? Write a welcome letter? Bake a cake? It was probably something he wasn't any good at, or else he'd have done it already . . .

"Map and card," Yuharu said under her breath.

"Oh. Yes. Right." Kohei nearly bonked his head on the doorframe in his hurry to leave. Yuharu sighed and tightened her grip on his ear. She was accustomed to his clumsiness, but that didn't mean she liked it.

Kohei might've been bad at card-writing and cake-baking, but he knew how to find his way around his own neighborhood, at least. He grabbed some paper and a dull pencil. What would the tenants need to know? The fastest route to the overpriced market, probably, and to the slightly better market, and the place tourists went to buy souvenirs, and the place they could buy *good* souvenirs. He remembered Mama mentioning that the new neighbors had a child his age, so he also tried to label the best ways to walk to school. There was a long way and a short way, but it was easy to confuse the long way to the *school* with the medium-length way to the *consulate* . . .

His welcome card was just another sheet of paper with a smiley face saying, "Omedetō!" Yuharu rolled her eyes and muttered something about his craftsmanship, but what else was a message like that supposed to say? The map was the important thing. You couldn't use a welcome card to find *food*.

Kohei presented his work to his mother, expecting her to at least be impressed with his map. But all she did was sigh, pinching the bridge of her nose. "Kohei-*ya* . . ." she said.

"I can make another card," Kohei reassured her. "But I didn't know what else I should—"

"The card is fine. But I told you to write the map's labels in English, remember? I could have made a Japanese version myself." Mama handed the papers back to him. "Just write out a second set of labels with arrows to show which word goes where."

"Oh," Kohei said. He glanced warily at Yuharu. "English?"

"You *have* been seeing your tutor every week, haven't you?"

"Yes, but—"

"Our new neighbors are moving from America. I think the mother's family was originally from Okayama, but the husband is a gaijin. Their daughter doesn't speak any Japanese at all."

"*Any?*" Kohei exclaimed.

"Please be gentle with her, Kohei. Imagine how frightening it would be to move to another country without

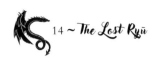

speaking the language. You would need a friend to help out, wouldn't you?"

"I guess so," Kohei admitted. "But if it were me, I wouldn't choose *me* to help me. I doubt I'd be much help to myself."

"You'll show her around at least?"

"Of course. But what if she—I dunno. What if she thinks I'm boring or something?"

Yuharu smothered a giggle. Kohei was tempted to yank her tail—she hated that—which reminded him . . .

"If I moved to a different country, I would probably just ask Yuharu to translate things," he said. "She's like a mini dictionary—a lot of ryū are."

"Merci, mon ami," said Yuharu.

"This American girl—will she not have a dragon of her own? Do Americans not . . . ?"

"The Carters have a dragon," Mama said, smoothing down a stray lock of her hair—the grayish one. "But it won't be a ryū, so it might not stay with the girl full-time. American families don't . . . well, they don't form multi-generational partnerships with entire dragon lineages the way we do with our ryū. They adopt their dragons like pets. And the Carters' is a rare type anyway . . ."

Mama said all of this very casually, like she was discussing plans for a pleasant outing next week, weather permitting, but only if you aren't busy, thank you very much.

Meanwhile, Kohei's entire world had just ground to a halt, turned upside down, and started spinning both ways simultaneously at breakneck speed.

A Western dragon?

A real one?

A big one?

Kohei had heard stories of Western dragons, usually with an assortment of knights and princesses thrown in— wyverns and firedrakes and lindwurms, all fierce beyond his wildest dreams. They were big. They were *beasts.* They'd probably never make snide comments about his hair.

And they could *fly.*

That impossible memory of the Western dragon circling the sky flashed in Kohei's mind: wide, powerful, bat-like wings; a snout with spikes instead of whiskers; the sleek, pointed nose of a predator. It surveyed the sprawl of the earth below like a falcon.

Would the new neighbors' American dragon be big enough to ride?

And . . . would Ojiisan like it?

Yuharu cleared her throat, tugging Kohei back into the real world. "Let's go finish that map, shall we?" she suggested. "Given the way you spelled 'boulevard' last week, I think the translations might take a while."

3
Not John Wayne

*K*ohei *knew from experience* that people in films were not the same as people in real life. He, for example, was neither a samurai nor a radioactive lizard monster. But part of him still half expected the new family—Sam and Reika Carter and their daughter, Isolde—to swagger down the streets of Ōsaka like they'd paved them themselves, glowing and grinning and calling out to strangers in a way that made friendliness seem a little bit like a threat. In movies, that's how Westerners were—they took up a lot of space, and the people around them didn't seem to mind as much as perhaps they should.

But the Carter family wasn't flashy or charismatic. The father was quiet, and the mother's eyes were shrewd but kind. They said a few hesitant words in Japanese as

Mama showed them around their new apartment, and Mama smiled to show them she understood. She spoke English less fluently than they spoke Japanese. Sometimes, Mr. Carter switched into Russian, which seemed to come to him easier; Mama understood him better that way too, but she didn't know enough of the language to respond. Kohei heard Papa's name mentioned a few times, along with "tovarisch," which Kohei thought meant *friend*. But he couldn't follow the conversation well enough to understand any more. Besides, the grown-ups weren't the main reason he was nervous.

Their daughter—*Isolde*, Kohei reminded himself—seemed intent on using her mother as a human shield. Mrs. Carter kept glancing over her shoulder, trying to nudge the girl out from behind her, muttering, "Isolde, ganbatte!" *Isolde, try.*

But Isolde never tried to introduce herself to Kohei, and Kohei never managed to catch more than a glimpse of his new friend. Was she scared of him? Was she hiding because she thought he was intimidating? Or threatening? The idea made Kohei feel prickly and guilty, half-ashamed and half-annoyed. He didn't want Isolde Carter to be frightened. They'd never even met before. What on Earth had *he* ever done to her?

To keep from fidgeting, he scanned the Carters' mostly empty apartment, wondering where the family would

keep their Western dragon. If it was as big as the ones he'd read stories about, it wouldn't even be able to *sit* in the kitchen without crushing the cabinets with its spiky tail. Maybe it was just a baby right now, and when it was grown, they'd move it to a stable in the countryside like a horse. Were there special stables designed specifically for dragons? Or could horses and dragons be roommates? They seemed like the kinds of species that wouldn't get along. Wouldn't the dragon *eat* the horses, like they did in fairytales?

Kohei wondered how long he should wait before asking all these questions. He didn't want his new neighbors to think that he only cared about them for their dragon.

"Kochirakoso," Mama said. "Dōmo," said Mrs. Carter. "Ī o-tenki," Mama said. "Sō desu ne," said Mrs. Carter.

Why were they talking about the *weather?* Why were adults always so interested in *nonsense?*

Finally, after what seemed like several decades of polite small talk, Mrs. Carter lost her patience. "Isolde!" she said, turning and dragging her daughter out into the open. She held the girl by the shoulders like she expected Isolde to make a run for it at the first opportunity. "Darling," she said in that slow, patient voice that grown-ups used when they were pretending they weren't frustrated. "Please greet your new neighbors. The way we practiced, remember?"

Isolde kept her head down so that all Kohei could see was the rough, dark waviness of her hair. "*Yrshikunegai-tashmsh*," she muttered.

"Um . . . yes. Welcome to your new home," Kohei replied politely, hoping that was the right response to whatever she'd just tried to say.

"Mmph," said Isolde. And that was that.

Mrs. Carter tried to get her daughter to talk a few more times, but it was obviously a lost cause. When the grown-ups settled down among the cardboard boxes to chat about ordinary things, Isolde stayed fixed in her spot as if she'd been frozen there. She kept her eyes looking down, like if she didn't acknowledge that Kohei was in front of her, he might stop existing before they actually had to say anything to each other. Kohei wanted to walk away—even meaningless chatter would be better than this awkward silence—but he felt weird leaving her there, so he stayed frozen like a statue too.

Would he have the courage to break the silence, or would they stand there until the apartment building was demolished in twenty years or so?

Okay, Kohei. He steeled himself and took a deep breath. *You can do this. You can be gracious and welcoming. Say something friendly in three . . . two . . . one . . .*

"Is it true that there are actually *five* members of the Beatles?" he blurted out in English.

It was a random, ridiculous thing to say, but at least it was ridiculous enough that Isolde had to look up in order to gape at him. Kohei was relieved to see she actually had a face. It was a warm, expressive face too, the kind that made it difficult for its owner to lie. *"Excuse* me?" she said in English.

"Eh . . . the Beatles," Kohei repeated. "The band from Great Britain, you know? John Lennon and Ringo Starr? Someone at school told me there are actually five of them, but two of them are identical, and they rotate positions every few concerts just to see if anyone will notice. And if anyone *does* notice, then they get to become the super-special *sixth* Beatle, king of *all* the Beatles."

Isolde's mouth hung half-open as she tried to make sense of all that. "I . . ." she began, then shook her head. "I just . . . ?" She paused. *"What?"*

The myth of the "Secret Beatle" was a rumor an older boy at Kohei's school had started spreading at the end of last year. Kohei knew it was too absurd to be true, but it was coming in handy now. Isolde was so busy wondering what he'd just said that Kohei finally had a chance to get a proper look at her.

She was taller than he was, with wavy, brown hair and a pointed chin. Her eyes had long, dark lashes, like Kohei's, but they were a lighter brown than his. She looked kind-of-sort-of-maybe-Japanese but not completely. And even though she'd spent most of the morning hiding behind her mother, Kohei knew from the way she studied him that she wasn't actually shy. Her eyes were curious and eager, even if she was afraid.

Other than that, he wasn't sure what to make of her. All he knew was that she was sizing him up too, and he hoped she didn't hate what she saw.

Once Isolde was done with her inspection, she exhaled, sticking her hand out like they were businessmen meeting for the first time. "Yoroshiku onegai itashimasu," she'd said, much clearer than the first time she'd tried.

Kohei grinned at her. Her pronunciation wasn't half-bad, though it was clear she had no idea what the greeting meant. "Yoroshiku," he said, grabbing her hand and shaking it. "Fujiwara Kohei to mōshimasu."

"Your name is . . . Fujiwara?" she repeated, frowning.

"Kohei. Call me Kohei. Fujiwara is my family name, so it comes first."

"Oh . . . right. Thanks." Isolde withdrew and wrung her hands, breathing deeply. She looked like someone who'd just jumped off a cliff into a rain forest—the rain forest was still terrifying, but at least she'd gotten the cliff part over with. "My name is Isolde Carter," she said. "Er . . . Carter *Isolde*. My mom says my Japanese name is Ayako, but, well . . ." She hunched her shoulders. "That's not *my* name, really."

Kohei nodded. "We had to learn French in school once, and my teacher called me *Étienne*," he said. "I always forgot to answer her."

"You speak French?"

"Only about as well as you speak Japanese."

Oh no, why would he *say* that? Thankfully, Isolde didn't seem too offended. In fact, she blushed like she was trying very hard not to laugh. "Well, your English is really good anyway," she said. "Almost as good as mine."

"Thank you. I have a tutor in the city." Kohei shrugged. "I'm not good at languages, but my ryū, Yuharu—she's upstairs right now—she's like a walking dictionary. I'm pretty sure she's half the reason ryū aren't allowed in the classrooms at school. She can't help blurting things out when other people don't answer quick enough."

"Yuharu?" Isolde said. Her brow creased as she mouthed the syllables, memorizing them. "*Yu-hah-roo.* That's cool. Our dragon's kind of the opposite—he's super shy, and he can barely even speak English."

"Oh?" Kohei's voice caught in his throat, and he tried not to sound too excited. *Their dragon.* He'd been so worried about how to bring it up in conversation, but now Isolde had gone and done it for him. "What language does he speak, then?"

"Yiddish," Isolde said. For the first time, something in her expression shifted, and she looked more proud than nervous. "Have you heard of it? It's like a cross between Hebrew and German and Polish, with a smidge of Russian thrown in. My dad says not many people speak it anymore, but Cheshire's grandfather belonged to my uncle, so . . ."

"Cheshire," said Kohei. "That's his name?"

"Yeah. After the cat from *Alice in Wonderland*, since he loves tea. I would've called him the Mad Hatter, but that didn't seem right, since he's *never* mean to rabbits. And he doesn't wear hats either." Isolde's words were starting to come faster—Kohei could still keep up with what she was saying, but he had a feeling he'd need Yuharu's help before long. "I think he'll like you. Do you want to meet him?"

"Oh, yes!" Kohei exclaimed.

Isolde beamed at him. "Neato!" she said. "I think my mom put his nest in my room, but I'm not sure. Is Yuharu upstairs? You should go and get her. Cheshire is shy, but maybe he'll like her, and it would be good for him to make some friends here . . ."

She dashed away before finishing her sentence. Kohei didn't mind, though. How could he? He was about to meet a real dragon.

Yuharu was indeed upstairs, lounging on the kitchen counter with Hana. Most ryū liked the sun—Hana was

curled up right by the window, her dusky scales catching the light—but Yuharu preferred the shade, so Kohei found her snoozing in her favorite spot behind Ojiisan's portable radio. "Come on," he said, scooping her up and tossing her onto his shoulder. "I met Isolde—she's going to show us her family's dragon."

"Is that so?" said Yuharu. She sounded annoyed—she always did when Kohei woke her up and jostled her around—but there was something else in her tone too.

Kohei didn't waste time wondering what it was. "Yeah," he said. "His name is Cheshire. Isolde's excited to show him to us. Apparently he speaks something called 'Yiddish.'"

"Oy vey," said Yuharu. Kohei braced himself for some sarcastic follow-up remark, but it never came. Yuharu was uncharacteristically quiet as they made their way back downstairs to the Carter family's apartment.

Isolde's parents were still conversing with Mama in their half-unpacked front room. Kohei wove his way through a maze of moving crates, trying not to disturb them even though his heart was jumping out of his skin with excitement. It didn't quite work—he tripped over a stack of textbooks at the edge of the room and staggered into an expensive-looking vase—but Yuharu caught it just in time. She glared at him. "You owe me," she hissed.

"Always," Kohei replied, slipping into the safety of the dark hallway.

Isolde's bedroom was actually designed to be a storage closet; Kohei's was too, but since his didn't have a sloped ceiling, it felt nearly twice the size. Their neighborhood had been constructed after the war, so the buildings stacked and stuck out like half-toppled alphabet blocks. They seemed to say, *The world doesn't make sense, so why should we?* At least the postwar houses in the countryside had vertical walls, and were neatly furnished with vinyl tatami mats and plexiglass shōji doors. Things were different here in the city. In their building, the angled staircase and twisty landing hallway jutted partway into the lower apartment, so Isolde didn't even have a window, just a lamp that she'd tilted sideways so it wouldn't bump up against the ceiling. How could a dragon of any size cram its nest into this tiny room? The only space Kohei could see was between Isolde's bed frame and a chest of drawers, and even a human would barely fit there.

"Uh . . . Isolde?" he said.

Isolde popped up from behind a large crate labeled *Heavier Books and Miscellany.* "Here!" she exclaimed. She shuffled sideways, trying to squeeze between two particularly large stacks of boxes without toppling them, and emerged with something clasped behind her back. "Ready to meet Cheshire?" she asked.

"Of course," Kohei said.

He felt like he was teetering on the edge of some towering precipice, and not in a good way—in a way that told

him he was about to be very disappointed. Whatever Isolde was about to reveal, it was small enough to fit in her hands. Kohei's optimistic side scrambled for hope: maybe Isolde was about to reveal a key to some large, rural stable, or a mysterious map showing him where her family's big dragon was *actually* building its den. That's what this was, right? It *had* to be.

Isolde grinned, paused for dramatic effect, then presented Kohei with the tiniest dragon he had ever seen.

It *was* definitely a Western dragon. It had bat-like wings and sharp spines, so different from Yuharu's long tufts of wavy fur. It also had four legs, sort of like a grass lizard. It might be able to breathe fire—enough to light a candle.

A *small* candle.

Kohei stared at the delicate, copper-scaled thing— *Cheshire*—and felt a hard lump in his throat. He was used to disappointment of all sorts, but really, this was ridiculous. It felt almost comedic. Like a studio audience would start laughing any second.

"Isn't he great?" Isolde said expectantly.

Kohei didn't dare open his mouth. If he so much as *breathed*, he would cry, and he did *not* want to cry.

"Like I said before, he doesn't speak much English," Isolde said. "He can understand it, though. You know how sometimes it's easier to listen to other people than it is to actually put sentences together? Plus, he's super-duper shy."

She tapped Cheshire's slender snout with her pointer finger, and the tiny dragon let out a pleased thrumming noise.

Oh, come on! It sounds like a pigeon!

Isolde looked up. "So, what will I do with him when we have to go to school?" she asked. "In New York, our principal decided that all dragons needed to be kept in crates if they came on school property. He thought they were a distraction—or maybe a fire hazard. Like a dragon could do more damage than my *classmates!*" She rolled her eyes. "Cheshire can't stand cages, so I would usually leave him at home with some snacks and the TV remote. We don't have a TV here, though, so—"

"There's a ryū den outside the school," Kohei muttered.

"Oh, close by? That's neat." Isolde gazed lovingly at Cheshire. "It'll be hard for him to make friends at first, but he'll figure it out eventually. Won't you, Chessie?" She tapped his nose again. "You could even learn Japanese."

Cheshire made a low huffing noise—he had his doubts.

"And this is Yuharu?" Isolde leaned forward, curious, to take a look at the ryū on Kohei's shoulder. "She's such a pretty color."

"Oh, thank you," Yuharu said, preening. Her tail traced happy figure-eights over Kohei's shoulder. "Kohei says he'd rather have a green or blue ryū, but I, for one, enjoy being pink."

The lump in Kohei's throat swelled. He wasn't angry. Was he angry?

Why would he be *angry?*

Isolde's room was dim, and the lopsided ceiling seemed like it was getting closer, drawing in tighter. Kohei took a deep breath and tried to conjure his impossible memory, the soft lightness of the ryū parade—that always calmed him down. Whenever he was agitated, all he had to do was trace Ojiisan's younger face in his mind and search for the raw glow of emotion, that bit of hope.

He tried to find the memory . . . but he couldn't.

For the first time in his life—the first time *ever*—that memory of the big ryū felt like any of his other memories, the ordinary ones. It was faded, not quite *there*. It was slipping from his fingers like rain steaming in the sun, like sand through a sieve, and he couldn't reach it, he couldn't keep it, couldn't hold onto it . . .

No, Kohei wasn't angry. He was frustrated. And it was better that way, because there was no one to be angry at, no one but himself, and if he was angry at *himself* . . .

"Kohei?" Isolde's voice floated to him from a great distance. She sounded concerned, like she'd tried several times to get his attention. "Are you all right? Are you, um . . . dai-joh-bu?"

Daijōbu.

That word. That stupid, stupid word. The lie Mama

repeated to herself every morning as she made breakfast: *it's okay, it's okay, don't worry, it's okay.* Kohei knew, logically, that Isolde didn't mean any harm. She was asking him if he was all right, not trying to convince him that he was.

But it was still that same, lingering word. A punch to the gut.

Kohei's hands balled into sweaty fists. "No," he said. "No, I am *not* okay!"

"Kohei-kun," Yuharu warned him. Some distant, logical part of Kohei knew she was right to warn him. None of this was Isolde's fault. The part of him that remembered to be reasonable watched the scene from a few inches above his head, and it saw that Isolde looked startled, frightened . . . and confused.

"Did I say it wrong?" she asked anxiously. "Dai—daijōbu. That means 'all right,' doesn't it? Is it offensive?" She looked to Yuharu. "What did I *do*?"

"You didn't do anything wrong," Yuharu reassured her. She slapped the side of Kohei's neck with her tail. He barely felt the sting of her scales against his skin. "Kohei, calm down."

"Urusai," Kohei replied through gritted teeth. *Annoying.* He wasn't sure what was wrong with him, but something was definitely wrong, and he didn't like it one bit. His skin was prickling, and he wanted to crawl out of it. He turned his gaze on Cheshire. "You too! Urusai nā!"

Neither Cheshire nor Isolde knew what that particular word meant, but Isolde seemed to have read Kohei's tone. She narrowed her eyes at him. "Excuse me?" she said. "Don't talk to him like that!"

It wasn't her fault. It certainly wasn't Cheshire's. It wasn't anybody's fault. The reasonable part of Kohei, still observing everything from above his actual head, clucked disapprovingly. *This isn't your fault either, Kohei*, it said, *but if you don't stop shouting at people, that might change.*

Yes, Kohei heard his voice of reason. But that voice wasn't stuck in a body that was boiling itself from the inside, and Kohei *was*, so he dismissed it with an irritated flick of his head. "Why shouldn't I shout at him?" he demanded. "What's he going to do, coo at me? He doesn't even speak any real languages!"

Isolde stiffened, cold flaring in her eyes. "Yiddish *is* real," she said.

"Kohei, apologize," Yuharu hissed. *"Now."*

Kohei was caught in that sort of frightened anger that made the floor seem faraway from his feet. "What's the point of a language no one else speaks?" he said. "And what's the point of a dragon that doesn't even—"

"Kohei!" Yuharu dug her claws into his shoulder, hissing. Kohei knew it should hurt, but he barely felt it. "Be quiet, *now!* What has gotten into you?"

Kohei didn't know.

And that was maybe the scariest part.

You've never actually yelled at anyone before, said the reasonable voice floating above his head. *And now you can't stop.*

What could ever make him stop?

Yamenaide, his father's voice had always said—*don't quit.* But now, it was yamerarenai—*can't* quit.

There is always good you can do, Kohei. Always.

Papa's voice. Woolen mittens on a cold, snowy day; a hug from someone who could make any problem go away with a smile and a squeeze of the shoulder.

Gaman. That's what Papa used to say when Kohei was frustrated. *Endure.* Endure, and persevere, and remember who you are.

Bit by bit, Kohei remembered that he was supposed to be breathing. Bit by bit, his mind began to reclaim fragments of that precious, impossible memory. His fists slackened, and his feet were flat on the ground again. His skin cooled.

He saw Ojiisan's young face in his mind—eyes, wide brow, clarity, *feeling.* Everything.

Reason lowered itself back into Kohei's mind, and it made him whole again.

Which, unfortunately, meant that he now had a clear view of Isolde's expression. And she wasn't scared anymore.

She was furious.

"How dare you?" she cried. "A language no one *speaks?* How could you—?" She gulped, with some difficulty.

"Cheshire," she continued, "is perfect." She sheltered the frightened little dragon in her arms, shielding him from Kohei. "He is absolutely perfect, and you don't deserve him, Kohei Fujiwara!" She peered down at her dragon, her gaze softening. "He's *mine.*"

Kohei didn't know what to say. He didn't know what to *do.* He backed away awkwardly, feeling around for the doorframe, and as soon as he knew Isolde couldn't see him, he turned and ran.

Next thing he knew, he was in his own apartment, sitting on his own bed. Yuharu had her claws dug into his right earlobe.

"Languages don't die unless the people who speak them are killed," she was saying. "Do you understand that?"

Not for the first time and not for the last, Kohei's lopsided apartment building felt like it was built only to collapse.

A man visited Kohei's dreams that night. It wasn't Ojiisan; if it were, Kohei would be able to see his face. The man in this dream was so tall, Kohei could barely see the shirt he was wearing.

Papa. Otōsan. Daddy. Next to him, Kohei was small, but not in a bad way. In a way that meant he didn't have to worry about all the big-and-complicated things that grown-up people needed to take care of. Those things were faraway, and Papa knew how to fix them. Papa would.

But then, like clouds thickening a sunny sky, something changed, and the tall presence disappeared.

And Kohei was still small, but now he was also cold.

The big, complicated things loomed over him. He couldn't see them.

He just knew he had to fix them.

4
First Days

Unfortunately for everybody in their general vicinity, Kohei and Isolde still had to be friends, regardless of whether or not they wanted to be. The first term of the school year began less than a week after the Carters arrived in their new home, and it wasn't like they could find someone else to guide Isolde until she learned enough Japanese to manage things by herself.

And she did need help. A lot of help. Not just with the language; Kohei was stunned by how how many things she simply didn't know.

According to Isolde, she was halfway through the fifth grade. Kohei tried to explain to her that fifth grade didn't start until the second week of April, but she kept insisting that it had begun in September, and her face crumpled in frustration when she couldn't convince him. She tried using Japanese, which didn't work. She'd get halfway through a sentence, then realize she'd begun in the middle of the thing she wanted to say. When she tried to start over at the beginning, she got flustered, which only made her more frustrated. While Kohei knew enough English to get a sense of what she was saying, he knew that very few of their classmates would.

Isolde knew it too. Kohei felt sorry for her at first, but it was hard to stay sorry for someone who hated his guts and wanted him to know it.

The day before their first term started, Isolde stopped talking altogether. She stopped *looking* at Kohei. That evening, when their two families got together for a home-cooked meal, she took the seat between her parents and kept her lips pressed shut no matter how many times Mama offered her a plate.

Cheshire kept murmuring to her, nuzzling her cheek and trying to console her.

Yuharu kept "accidentally" hitting the nape of Kohei's neck with her tail, just to make sure he remembered that everything was his fault.

If she was trying to make him feel guilty, Kohei reflected, it wasn't working. Well, it *was*, in a way—he hadn't stopped wallowing in shame since their one-sided argument about Cheshire. But since he was already as sad

as he could be, getting hit repeatedly in the neck just made him annoyed. He tried not to look at Isolde, then felt bad for ignoring what he'd done to her. So he looked at her, but she was two seats away from Ojiisan, which meant he could see both of the people he'd disappointed that week in a single glance.

The prickly, guilty feeling was coming back.

No thoughts, Kohei-kun. No anger. Just focus on your plate and try to eat. Don't think about Isolde. Don't even think about Ojiisan. Just don't, just don't, just—

"Mr. Fujiwara? Mr. . . . um . . . Fujiwara-san?" Isolde's mother sounded concerned. She'd leaned across her husband and daughter to peer at Ojiisan's face, which, to Kohei's horror, had gone the color of watered-down milk.

"Ojiisan?" said Kohei, half rising from his seat.

Ojiisan muttered something, his grip tightening on his spoon. He hadn't touched his broth at all.

"You feeling all right, sir?" Isolde's father asked. He was the only person sitting next to Ojiisan, though Mama and Mrs. Carter were directly opposite.

Ojiisan squeezed his eyes shut as all the blood drained from his face. "Shikata ga nai," he said. *There is nothing that can be done.*

Kohei stiffened. He searched for his father's voice in his mind—*yamenaide, don't quit*—but he couldn't find it, and its absence left him speechless.

Everything turned loud and clattery as the grown-ups dropped their bowls and utensils and hurried to tend to the old man. Isolde stayed seated, but her stony facade faltered, and she loosened her arms, watching uncertainly as the events unfolded.

Kohei couldn't move. He couldn't. Everything whirled in his mind: the silence of his father's voice, the frantic concern on Ojiisan's face when Kohei fell down the stairs, the absent parts of his impossible memory, the urgency in his mother's voice across the table, the sound of Yuharu saying something he could barely hear—and more than anything, the hurt in Isolde's eyes when he'd yelled at her, even though he hadn't meant to make her upset, even though he'd never *wanted* to.

Ojiisan was sick. Ojiisan was going to die. The next time Kohei fell down a set of stairs, nobody would come for him.

Well, Mama might. But she would just say that awful, awful word—daijōbu—as if repeating it over and over again could somehow make it true.

Isolde's first day in a Japanese school was also Ojiisan's first day in the hospital. Kohei no longer felt prickly—he felt numb, which was almost worse. His entire mind was in

the hospital, at his grandfather's bedside. He didn't see the point of hiding that from his "friend."

At the very least, Isolde's mood was tempered by her concern for Kohei's family. She made a real effort to act like she wasn't angry at Kohei anymore; she even tried to smile as they approached the ryū den tucked behind the school building. "Oh, wow! Look at all those cute pillow nests," she exclaimed, stooping to read the wooden welcome sign the first-years had decorated the previous year. "Ryū . . . no . . . su. Does that mean dragons' den?" She looked up at Kohei, waiting for an answer.

She didn't get one.

"Oh. Well, um . . . kakkoī-na," she said, straightening up. *Really cool.*

Kohei could've told her that pretending to be friends never worked when only one person was trying.

They'd arrived a bit early, at Mrs. Carter's suggestion— all the grown-ups had agreed that it would be better for Isolde to see the building before the first-day surge of students crowded the front grounds. Kohei had to admit that seemed like a good idea. Even without tons of new people surrounding her, Isolde looked nervous. She was wearing her brand-new uniform, complete with a school hat that was definitely too big for her. It sagged over her forehead and made her look younger. Kohei knew it would only get worse when the stiff fabric began to soften.

His own uniform was much more worn-in. The hat fit perfectly and his sleeves were the proper length. Isolde kept tugging at her high collar, which made Kohei wonder whether schools in New York even required uniforms. They didn't use indoor shoes, something Isolde had made very clear during their long walk to school.

"But what if someone steals my actual shoes?" she'd asked him a thousand times.

"They won't."

"They won't? How do you know?"

"They *won't*."

Kohei was tired of explaining things. Especially obvious things. He shouldn't even be at school—he belonged at Ojiisan's side, watching over him, making sure everything was okay, because he knew that Mama couldn't handle it. She would *pretend* things were fine, and she'd sweep all the broken pieces out of sight, but if something went wrong, if things turned really, really bad—

"Kohei?" Isolde had settled Cheshire inside the ryū den with Yuharu, but she was fidgeting with the hem of her blazer like she was nervous to leave him. "Um . . . do we need to go somewhere?"

Kohei shook his head. "We can wait a bit," he said. "There are a few benches by the gates, and other people should be arriving soon."

"Will we meet anyone?" said Isolde.

Kohei blinked at her. "Meet?" he echoed.

"Like . . . are we going to meet up with your friends before we go inside?"

It was an innocent question, and Isolde looked so earnest. Kohei kind of felt bad for her. "I don't exactly have friends," he admitted.

"Why not?" Isolde's face went carefully blank. "That's awful. Did they switch to a different school?"

Kohei shook his head. "They're still here," he said. "And I guess they're not *not* my friends. They're just not interested in me anymore. I'm fine with it."

Isolde's brow was creased in confusion, but she nodded anyway, somehow sensing that Kohei didn't want to face any more questions right now.

Neither of them wanted to sit down. Kohei found himself wandering up and down the length of the gray school building, and Isolde gladly followed him. She didn't seem to enjoy walking in silence, though. "Kohei," she said, taking off her too-big school hat. "Can we talk?"

"Mmph," said Kohei. He kept his eyes trained ahead.

"I think we need to. We can't take turns being angry at each other all year. And you're—I mean, it's not like I have anyone else I can talk to about anything, right?" She paused. "Kohei?"

"Mmph," Kohei said again. It was the most-used word

in Ojiisan's vocabulary, and he was beginning to appreciate its versatility.

Isolde bowed her head. "Please," she said. "I just need to know. Why did you yell at me that first time we met?"

"Uh-huh," said Kohei. Tears began to sting his eyes. *Please don't ask me about that, please don't make me think about it, don't make me cry, I don't* want *to cry . . .*

"Was it something I said? Whatever it was, I didn't mean it."

"Mm."

"I'm serious!" Isolde's voice strained. "It's really hard, you know! I don't know anything here. I mean, I know some words, and I know what they mean, but I don't know what they *mean.* I don't know what will offend people, and I'm sorry if I hurt you, but it wasn't on purpose, and it's not fair for you to hurt *me* on purpose when I didn't try to do anything wrong!"

Kohei felt like his heart was being squeezed, which only made him more determined to avoid talking about things that might make him cry. The tears felt threateningly close, now—he was holding something powerful and dangerous by a very thin rein.

He started to walk faster.

"Kohei." Isolde jogged to catch up with him. "Please, please don't run away from me. I'm sorry! Just tell me what I'm doing wrong!"

"Nothing!" Kohei croaked. "It's not you!"

"Then what is it? What can I do?"

"You can't do anything."

"Why not?"

Kohei wheeled around to glare at her, and she almost crashed straight into him before jumping back. "Because *I* will," he said. "I'll fix everything. I just need time to think—to come up with a plan."

"Oh." Isolde frowned. "Wouldn't talking about it help you think?"

"Why would it?"

"I dunno." She hunched her shoulders, her gaze dropping to the cracks in the pavement. "It helps *me*. Sometimes, when I have a big problem, I talk it through out loud, and things make much more sense."

"Oh." Kohei took a deep breath. "Well—no, I don't think that will help me. But thank you."

Isolde still didn't look up at him.

"And I'm sorry for insulting Cheshire," Kohei added. "I didn't know how important Yiddish is to your family . . . and I shouldn't have yelled. I'm sorry."

Isolde didn't say anything.

When Kohei finally found the courage to look up at her face, he expected to see her glaring at him, her anger renewed. Instead he was faced with an exasperated smile.

"That's *literally* all you needed to say," Isolde said. "You make things harder for yourself than they need to be, you know that?" She glanced over her shoulder. "Also, I think our classmates are starting to arrive."

The school had been informed about Isolde. The administration knew her name, knew the languages she spoke, and had a full record of her performance at her school in New York.

But they didn't quite know what to do about her hair.

The headmaster's assistant thought that Isolde had broken the dress code by using a curling iron—which she hadn't—but Isolde didn't know the word for "hair" or for "curly," and she kept accidentally saying "hospital" instead of "hairdresser," which only made things worse. She stood with her chin pressed into her chest, her shoulders hunched stiffly so that her new randoseru backpack rode halfway up her neck. She looked like a turtle who wished it had a thicker shell. The headmaster and his assistant and a handful of teachers, attracted by the noise, stared at her in polite bewilderment, frowning amongst themselves.

Eventually, Kohei stepped in to testify on her behalf, and the headmaster nodded in understanding. His assistant

made a brief note on her clipboard, shooting an apologetic smile at Isolde; they'd made dress code accommodations for curly-haired students before, but it wasn't common.

It was a small bump in the road, as far as Kohei was concerned. Isolde disagreed. She continued to look like a harried turtle for the rest of the day, and every time something unfamiliar surprised her—the morning aerobics, the classroom cleaning duties, the fact that she wasn't supposed to bring her own lunch—she seemed to become even more intent on willing a protective shell into existence. It was so sad to watch, Kohei almost forgot about the fact that Ojiisan was still sick, still fighting organ failure in the hospital.

Almost. Not quite.

Isolde attracted some curious looks from their classmates. One girl frowned suspiciously, while another gazed longingly at the waves of Isolde's hair. Both were harmless, as Kohei tried to tell her. Isolde didn't respond.

Two of the stares were for Kohei. Those were harder to ignore.

Tadashi L. Ueda and Hisao Abe were Kohei's friends. *Sort* of. Kohei wasn't entirely sure where they stood anymore. When they were younger, they were like three peas in a pod—they had done everything together. And to the best of Kohei's knowledge, he hadn't done anything in particular to change that.

Still, Tadashi and Hisao had become less and less interested in Kohei over the past few years. Maybe they
thought he was annoying now, or too immature, or maybe
just *boring.*

When Kohei walked into the classroom with Isolde
sulking at his heels, the other two peas looked interested
in him again. But it wasn't a good kind of interested.
They were watching him like he was an experiment and
they were the scientists—whatever they were whispering to each other, it was clear they didn't want him to
join in.

He tried not to look at them. Isolde tried not to look
at *anybody.* It was easy enough for both of them when they
were in class, since most of Kohei's energy was spent trying to do things like remember the English word for
sankaku ("You know, the—the *three* shape! Like a pointy
square!"). But when everyone flooded toward the ryū den
at dismissal time, Tadashi and Hisao swooped in.

"Is she your new friend, Arahata?" Hisao asked in
Japanese. He was smaller than Tadashi and Kohei, but he'd
always made up for it with his carefully chosen words—he,
more than anyone else Kohei knew, used honorifics and
polite speech as a weapon.

Which meant that the teasing way he said *Arahata*—
Kohei's father's surname—made Kohei bristle, balling his
hands into fists on instinct. "Yes," he said. "Yes, she is."

Tadashi, the tallest of the three boys, stepped sideways to stand between Kohei and the entrance to the ryū den. Isolde shifted uneasily—she couldn't have understood exactly what Hisao said, but she could tell that something was wrong. "Kohei?" she whispered.

Kohei ignored her. "We'd like to get through," he told Tadashi.

"We'd like to talk," Hisao said.

"About what?"

Hisao tipped his head at Isolde.

"What about me?" Isolde demanded in English. She looked between Kohei and his former friends. "What are you talking about? Why did he just—?"

"What's there to talk about?" Kohei asked.

"You shouldn't be her friend," Tadashi blurted out. His brown hair was more neatly combed than Hisao's, but he never bothered combing his words.

"Is that so?" Kohei said.

Isolde elbowed him. "*Hey*," she hissed. "Can you please talk slower?"

"We're just a little concerned," Hisao said. "We think you may not be the best *influence* on her."

"Excuse me?"

"Don't deny it!" Tadashi exclaimed. "We know what kind of a person you are—my mother told me what your family's like."

"I have no idea what you're talking about," Kohei told him.

Hisao scoffed. "You don't *know?*"

"For real?" said Tadashi.

"Yes, for real! I have no idea what you're talking about! Is this why you've stopped talking to me? I haven't done anything wrong!"

"My mother told me you'd deny it!"

"Hisao, I swear—"

"SHUT . . . *UP!*" Isolde shrieked. "Please, I—I know you're talking about me, and you're angry, but I *don't know what you're saying!* Just stop for one second! *Please!*"

Everyone around them—even the ryū in the den, even the littlest kids—fell silent. One tiny girl with a missing front tooth stared at Isolde. The taller boy holding her hand looked afraid.

Isolde shrank into herself again, even though a moment ago she'd been shouting. It was quiet now. Maybe she hadn't meant to make so much noise, and now the silence sounded like an accusation.

Her face crumpled, and she pushed past Tadashi. Tadashi looked stunned, but Hisao looked smug. *That was your fault, Kohei*, his gaze said, like that made any sense.

Kohei gave him a withering look and went to follow Isolde. She had caught sight of Cheshire, perched on the

root of a nearby tree just outside the den. "Chess?" she said, kneeling to greet him. "You okay?"

Cheshire tipped his head from side to side, making a face. Isolde laughed. Kohei knew that laughter was supposed to be a good thing, but there was a thickness to Isolde's voice that made him think she was trying not to cry. "Well," she said. "It'll be a relief to get h-*home* anyway."

Kohei set Yuharu on his shoulder, unsure of what he should do. Should he console her? Beat up Hisao and Tadashi? Honestly, he wasn't sure why Isolde was so upset. Was she tired? He supposed he couldn't blame her for that.

When Isolde turned around, there weren't any tears on her face. In fact, she was smiling again, a little too brightly. "I'm totally fine," she said. "Let's get going, okay?"

5
What Friends Are For

"*Tadaima!*" *Kohei called,* letting his school bag slip to the floor. "Mama? I'm home!" He looked around. "Where are you?"

She was in the kitchen, slumped in her seat at the dining table.

There was no *daijōbu*, no weary smile, no sweeping the usual fragments of broken glass out of sight. Mama had spent the entire morning at the hospital. Her hair had fallen half out of its usual bun, and she had a mug of tea cradled in her hands. It was completely full, like she'd forgotten she was supposed to drink it.

Kohei hovered in the doorway, feeling oddly like an intruder in his own home. Yuharu set a comforting paw on the nape of his neck, but he barely felt it.

When Mama looked up at him, her gaze settled on his face the way dust might caress an empty shelf. "Okaeri," she said. "I'm glad you're home."

Silence.

She set her mug on the table. "Kohei," she said quietly. "Would you like to see him?"

Isolde was sitting on the floor just outside her family's apartment, Cheshire cradled in her lap. Kohei shot a quizzical look at the two of them as Mama came down the stairs behind him. Isolde shrugged in response. "Where are you going?" she asked him.

"The hospital," Kohei said shortly. "My grandfather."

"Oh." Isolde struggled to her feet. "Do you want me to come with you? For moral support?"

"That's very kind of you," Mama said, "but it won't be a pleasant visit. You don't need to put yourself through it for our sake."

"But that's what friends are for!" Isolde turned to Kohei, sympathetic and grim and understanding all at once. "You don't need to be alone, you know. You really don't."

Kohei had never felt more grateful to anyone in his life, though he knew Isolde was probably just looking for an excuse not to tell her parents about her day.

The hospital wasn't far from their neighborhood, but they still took a bus. Mama wasn't the only one who was too tired to walk. Isolde had never used public transit in Japan before, but she pretended she wasn't scared for Kohei's sake. It was crowded enough to suffocate someone. Mama stood, clinging to one of the overhead rings; Kohei and Isolde squeezed into one seat while Yuharu and Cheshire perched on a nearby ledge.

Kohei still felt like an intruder in his body, like a ghost floating two inches above the ground. He watched himself from a distance the way he watched the almost-evening sky through the rattling bus window across the aisle.

He wasn't sure if he ever wanted to feel real again.

The hospital lurched into view. It had been renovated right after the war, repainted and reinforced. The structure had been compromised by repeated bombings, so most of the building was newly constructed.

Still, there were patches where old injuries showed through: walls that hadn't been completely bleached, wood beams with scorch marks still visible from certain angles. Once upon a time, Kohei's father had told him that hospitals were like war zones, and sometimes even harder to forget.

Papa would have known better than anyone. He'd been a doctor. He'd worked long hours, early mornings, late nights, at this very hospital.

In this very ward.

And he'd been taken to this ward the night he died too. He'd slipped right through his colleagues' fingers.

Kohei swallowed the lump in his throat, trying to find his father's voice in his mind. *Yamenaide, yamenaide. Ganbatte ne, Kohei. Don't quit, don't quit. Keep trying, Kohei . . .*

Papa's voice, deep and warm—the sound of protection. Kohei clung to that sound with all his might as the attending physician and a spindly surgeon-ryū led him, Mama, and Isolde to Ojiisan's hospital bed.

He was in one of the older wings, one that had survived the worst of the shells. It was grayer than the rest of the building, all plaster and exposed boards, a startling amount of damaged wall peeking through the thick, plastic dividing curtains. Funny, Kohei thought in a detached sort of way, how the buildings that were spared total destruction during the war ended up looking the shabbiest when the rebuilding was done. Things that seemed *okay* were never looked at too closely.

Ojiisan was propped up on a stained linen pillow. His skin, clammy and tinged gray, looked a lot like the compressed sponge mattress beneath him. He was awake, but his eyelids hung low with fatigue—he observed his surroundings through his lashes.

He was barely moving. Kohei spotted the mechanical rise and fall of his chest, but it was shallow.

Kohei's own insides were collapsing in on themselves too.

He stood in the doorway while Mama went to the bed, leaned down, and whispered something in her father's ear. Ojiisan's eyelids flickered in—what, recognition? It was hard to say. His face didn't change. He muttered something in response, but it was too low to hear. Isolde glanced at Kohei, questioning; Kohei glanced at Yuharu, who shook her head.

Kohei felt his father's hand in his. The strength and callouses of a bigger hand closed around his own. A squeeze for courage. "Gaman, gaman," his father had whispered, sensing the terror that thrummed through Kohei's three-year-old soul the first time he came in for a checkup. "Endure. Head high. Dignity and perseverance. You are more than the world will ever know."

"WHY?" Ojiisan roared.

In English.

Oh, no.

Isolde jerked back, nearly toppling over in a panic. Kohei grabbed her arm on instinct, but other than that, he was paralyzed.

His grandfather tried to lunge forward, but he couldn't sit up very far. He fell back helplessly, glaring at Mama, then up at the ceiling as several doctors rushed in, followed by ryū whose hollow claws were used as

syringes. Ojiisan waved them away, pursing his lips tight.

Mama folded her arms defensively. "He needs to see you," she said to her father. "It could be the last chance you have—"

"You should not have brought him."

"He's your grandson, and you need to—"

"You must take him away!"

A dull ache caught in the back of Kohei's throat, a tight sort of despair that squeezed the air from his lungs.

They were talking about him.

His ojiisan didn't want to see him.

Mama was angry, and Kohei could tell she wanted to yell back. But she couldn't. So all the anger rushed to her cheeks as heat and tears, and she pinned her hands under her elbows like she was worried she might hit something, and Ojiisan was *livid*, and it was all because of Kohei.

He was a burden here. He should not have come.

But what had Mama said?

This could be the last chance you have.

The distant, floating feeling was gone. Kohei's mind was very much back in his body, but he still couldn't quite feel anything—or maybe he was feeling everything, which was just as overwhelming. His skin was boiling—or maybe he was cold. He was sweating—or maybe the tingling in his fingers meant he didn't exist at all.

Someone's hand was on his arm. It wasn't Papa's. It wasn't a strong hand, just a firm one.

"Come on," Isolde murmured. "Let's get some air."

Kohei would have protested, but he heard Yuharu say something soothing, and even though he didn't understand any of her words, he knew that he should leave.

The last thing Ojiisan said as Isolde tugged Kohei into the cool quietude of the hallway was loud enough to crack the world.

"He is too young! You cannot let him see this—what kind of a mother are you?"

Isolde forced Kohei to sit down on a bench in the hall. She left Cheshire beside him and flitted out of Kohei's field of vision. Slowly, as the rushing in his ears began to fade, Kohei realized that Yuharu was still talking.

"He cares about you, your family loves you, they want you to be happy," she soothed him. "This happens. People say things they don't mean sometimes, but it's okay. It'll be fine."

Kohei had been so hot a minute ago. Now he was shivering, and his bones felt all hollowed out. "Don't say that," he said.

"Don't say what?" said Yuharu.

"You're using different words, but I know what you *mean*." He glared at her as she settled on his shoulder, her tail curled lightly over the back of his neck. "You're saying, 'shikata ga nai.' You're saying there's nothing we can do."

Yuharu opened her mouth like she wanted to say something, then thought better of it and shook her head.

Isolde appeared again, a little paper cup of water in her hand. "Here," she said breathlessly, offering it to Kohei. "I practically had to wrestle a security dragon for this." She hesitated, looking Kohei over. "Are you okay?"

Kohei didn't answer.

"Not, like, emotionally. I mean, are you about to collapse?"

Kohei shook his head.

"Well . . . that's good." Isolde scooped Cheshire into her arms and lowered herself at Kohei's side. "Do you want to talk about all this?"

Kohei closed his eyes. "Why?" he said.

"Because talking helps. Things always seem simpler when you say them out loud. And eventually, you stop talking, and you realize that if your sentence can end, so can your troubles."

"She's right, Kohei," Yuharu murmured. "It will help to talk."

The shivering hadn't stopped. Now a wave of pressure

rose through Kohei's body. He feared that if he opened his mouth to say anything, a dam would break and he would be washed away by a force he couldn't understand.

He needed to move. He didn't need to talk—he needed to *fix* this.

The hospital was whirring steadily around him.

What would Papa have done?

Yamenaide. Yamenaide . . .

Papa would not quit.

Kohei rose. "Papa's office," he croaked.

"What about it?" Yuharu asked.

"It's exactly the way it was when he—I mean, Mama's never touched it. His papers are still there." Kohei had started walking without even realizing it. Yuharu had her talons buried in the fabric of his shirt collar. Isolde was half jogging to catch up. "Papa will know what to do!"

"Do what?" Isolde demanded. "Kohei, wait!"

Kohei stopped suddenly, whirling around to face her. "To make a big dragon," he said. "That will make Ojiisan happy—to find a big dragon. That'll make him smile, even—even if it's for the very last time!"

He turned and stormed away before anyone could tell him to calm down or think.

Isolde was still on Kohei's heels as they entered their apartment building, was still trying to talk him out of it when he burst into Papa's old office. "This is ridiculous!" she exclaimed, snatching Yuharu from Kohei's shoulder just as the little ryū lost her grip on his shirt. "Kohei, slow *down!*"

Kohei went straight to Papa's bookshelf, looking for something, *anything*. A sign. Mama dusted the shelves and the desk sometimes, when she was lonely or angry, but other than that, everything was in its usual place: the pot in the corner that was crammed full of textbooks instead of plants, the threadbare carpet that seemed woven from dust. This room made Kohei feel like Papa had only just left, like all his papers and journals were still waiting patiently for him to return.

The room was mittens on a cold day, the roughness of a thick woolen cloak—it was all the things that Papa always was.

Kohei took a deep, steadying breath.

Most of the books were thick and leather-bound, the kind of heavy tomes that you couldn't check out from a public library. Reference materials. Some were a more manageable size—thin enough to bend, with paper that was as flimsy as newsprint. Kohei had tried to read those when he was younger, but the words were so tiny and crowded on the page. It was the kind of text that only a grown-up would even think of reading, and he doubted they'd be any less intimidating now. He ran his fingers over the thin spines, wondering.

Then a dull, metallic glint on the top shelf caught his eye.

Papa's favorite lighter. It was an old, elegant, almost-antique model, silvery and smooth to the touch. Papa had always kept it out of Kohei's reach when he was a baby, since babies love grabbing at shiny things. But Kohei was tall enough now that he could reach it if he stood on his toes. It was dusty, but once he wiped it off with his shirt, it was just as glossy and silver as he remembered.

And the inscription was still there—two kanji that Kohei had memorized long before he was old enough to learn to read or write:

怪我

They were strange characters to carve into a precious object. As soon as he knew how to use a dictionary, Kohei had looked up their meanings: they were pronounced "kega," the Japanese word for *injury*. At the time, he'd wondered if it was a warning that fire could be dangerous. But the stamp on the bottom said that the lighter was sterling silver, an expensive thing to bother having engraved

with something so ordinary, especially in the midst of a war.

Kega. Something that hurt, maybe more badly than fire.

Kohei weighed the lighter in his palms. It was heavy and cool, like a metal stone. He'd loved it so much when he was little. Papa carried it in his pocket every day when he was alive, and Kohei remembered asking over and over again to see the "fast fire." He'd liked how quickly the flame flicked up, and how easy it was to make it go away.

"Kohei!" Isolde's sharp tone interrupted his peaceful thoughts. "Are you even listening to me?"

Kohei had forgotten she was there. He turned to her, still clutching his father's lighter in both hands. "What?" he said.

"Tell me what you're doing. Now." Isolde stuck her chin out. "*I* am putting my foot down!"

The kanji inscription on Papa's lighter seemed to wink at Kohei. *It hurts*, it said, like it was trying to remind him of something. *Kega . . .*

Kohei exhaled slowly. "It's complicated," he said. "Very complicated."

"Most important things are." Isolde looked him straight in the eye.

She wasn't wrong.

So Kohei looked away from her face, and he told her everything.

Isolde didn't laugh at him like he'd half expected her to. She didn't look angry when he told her that he'd been disappointed by Cheshire either. She mostly looked sad. "So that's why you got mad at me," she said. "You were disappointed that Cheshire wouldn't make your grandpa happy again." She set Yuharu on Papa's desk, wanting to cup Cheshire in both hands. "It wasn't because *daijōbu* is a bad word?"

"*Daijōbu* isn't *bad*," Kohei said. His chest was lighter—he almost felt giddy. "It's just that people say it to me all the time, and it's never true, that's all."

Isolde's shoulders sagged in relief. "Oh, good," she said. "I was so sure I'd accidentally insulted you, or something."

"It would've been funny if you had. I say bad words in English all the time, completely by accident. My tutor hates it, so I've been keeping track of the really awful ones for future reference."

Isolde giggled. *Strange*, Kohei thought—it was like he could see her now, actually *see* her, for the very first time. And for better or for worse, she could see him in return.

"Okay," Isolde said, pushing her hair out of her face. "So, you think that your grandfather needs to see a big dragon in order to remember how to be happy again. Is that right?"

Kohei nodded. "I always thought I'd go on some epic quest when I was older to find one for him," he said. "But now . . ."

Now, *when I was older* wasn't a possibility. The whole world had shifted, and Kohei didn't know where he was going, or why he was still where he was.

Isolde nodded grimly. "Right," she said. "And you think your dad's papers might have something helpful in them?"

"I don't know. Maybe." Kohei looked around the room at all the bookshelves and paper-stuffed file folders, labeled in his father's neatly inked handwriting. "Or maybe I just feel safe here."

He held out his hand so that Yuharu could climb back up his arm and onto his shoulder where she belonged. She settled herself with as much dignity as she could muster. "Well, I *do* think your father researched ryū morphology in his free time," she said in English. "My brother told me about it a long time ago, though I didn't pay much attention."

"Ryū morphology?" Kohei echoed. "I don't know that second word."

"'Morph' means *to change*, and '-ology' is *the study of*," Isolde said, pleased to be able to show off her language skills for once.

"The Latin root 'morph' actually just means *shape* or *form*," Yuharu said.

Isolde gave her a dirty look. "Whatever."

"Do you know if he wrote any of his research down, Yuharu?" Kohei asked.

Of course he had. Papa wrote *everything* down. So even though everyone was too tired to think straight, and Kohei and Isolde had school tomorrow and lots of homework left to do, they settled down right then and there to dig through all of Papa's books and notes and notebooks. They each had a specific job: Cheshire sorted materials into piles by size, Isolde handled the texts that were in English, Kohei took the Japanese ones, and Yuharu worked on translating everything else. Papa had known a lot of languages, so there were books scattered here and there that were written in French, Russian, and what Yuharu claimed was ancient Sumerian.

The edge of panic had worn off, and Kohei no longer felt like he was racing the clock. It wasn't that the sense of importance had faded—just that the panic had settled and hardened into something steadier but so much more potent.

No more fear now—just determination. Kohei had people by his side, and he was never going to quit.

There was always good he could do.

6
Old Books

*M*ama *didn't come home* until a little past midnight. She must've assumed that Kohei was already in bed, because she didn't bother to check on him before falling asleep herself . . . which was good, because by a little past midnight, Papa's office looked like it had been carefully dissected by a half-dozen hurricanes.

They'd sorted everything into piles. The further they got, the fewer Japanese texts they found, which meant that Yuharu's stack of foreign-language books was almost the tallest in the room—more Polish, more German, more French. There were so few English books, Isolde finished early and took a nap on a bed of scientific journals. Yuharu, a quick reader and a lover of sleep, joined her before long.

They woke to find Kohei encased in his fortress of

manuscripts, puzzling over a small pamphlet bound in red cloth and thread.

"What's that?" Yuharu asked, stretching her wings and crawling over his shoulder to take a look.

"I don't know," Kohei muttered. "It's in English, but it's weird. The words don't make sense."

"Oh?" Yuharu peered at it, then let out a hoot of laughter. "That's not *English*, Kohei, it's Russian!"

"Oh, is it?" Kohei scowled at her. "How was I supposed to know?"

"They don't even use the same alphabet!"

He shrugged, trying to dislodge her from her perch on his shoulder. "Fine," he said. "But for the record, *you* were supposed to take care of the Russian books."

"I know. I must have missed one." The little ryū clambered down his arm. "This one doesn't look like it'll be helpful anyway. See that ink stamp on the front? It's a dissertation from the university's history department. Your father's colleagues were always asking him to review their projects, and he felt guilty about turning them away . . ."

Isolde managed to sit up, rubbing her eyes and pushing her hair out of her face. "What is it?" she asked through a yawn. "Did you find anything useful?"

"Maybe." Kohei shook his head and set the small, not-English book aside. "I don't understand a lot of Papa's books, but some of them have notes in the margins—in his

handwriting." Wistfulness threatened to knock him right over. "I recognized it."

"Oh." Isolde crawled to his side of the room. "Anything about dragons?"

"Yes." Kohei reached for one of the larger books, bound in green. "This one has a *lot* of notes in it."

It was *A Study of Ryū Genetics* by Dr. Hisoka Arima, a name Kohei recognized immediately, though he hadn't heard it in years. Dr. Arima had come to visit a lot in the weeks after Papa died. He would stand on their front step and ring the doorbell over and over again—Kohei remembered how Mama would lock everything to try to keep him from getting in.

"He was an old friend of your father's," she'd told Kohei, leaning her shoulder against the front door like it was a barricade. "They went to school together, but they fell out during the war. Your father never trusted him again."

It took weeks before Dr. Arima gave up. But he left one final note for Mama—his home address, telephone number, and a single phrase: *For when the boy needs a real father.*

Kohei opened *A Study of Ryū Genetics* cautiously, like it might explode. But it was only a book.

Papa had annotated almost every single line.

His handwriting was so tiny, it was difficult to read in

the dim light. But every few chapters, a paragraph or two were marked with a set of very familiar kanji:

怪我

Just like on Papa's lighter, which Kohei still had tucked away in his jacket pocket.

"The sections Papa marked are mostly scientific stuff," he explained, flipping through so that Isolde could see. "I don't understand them very well."

"Enzymes . . . homeothermic status, thermolabile," Yuharu read aloud. "Deoxyribonucleic acid . . ."

"Oh wait! I know that one!" Isolde exclaimed.

Everyone, including Cheshire, gaped at her in disbelief.

"No, seriously. Deoxyribo . . ." She waved her hand dismissively. "That thing Yuharu said. It's the full name for DNA. My science teacher told me about it when I lived in New York."

"DNA," said Kohei. He had heard of that too. It had been discovered around the time he was born—genetic information that could be passed down through generations. DNA was the reason Ojiisan was small but Mama was tall, and why Kohei was left-handed, not right-handed. It was a little bit lovely—DNA was a link between Kohei and his oldest, most distant ancestors.

But it was also frightening. Because if Kohei got his DNA from Ojiisan, it meant he might end up in the same place when he was older: miserable, sick, and angry at everything in the world.

"Does it say anything about big ryū?" he asked Yuharu.

"Hmm . . ." Yuharu nudged his hands away from the page so she could flip between chapters. "Maybe. Look, right here—*heat*."

She was pointing at another one of the passages Papa had marked with kanji, one that was written so simply, even Kohei could understand it. "Heat," he said. He looked up at Isolde, the unfamiliar glow of hope spreading through his body. "Exposing a ryū egg to *heat* will make the hatchling bigger."

"Seriously?" Isolde said. "It's that easy?"

"Hmph." Yuharu was hesitant—not scared, exactly, but not excited, either. "I've heard of the heat trick. It was a hot-button issue back in the day."

"Is it dangerous?" Isolde asked.

"No. The debates were more over philosophy and ethics. Traditionally, Shintoism doesn't approve of meddling with nature. That's why Japanese dogs are practically wolves—no one's tried to make them into golden retrievers yet."

Kohei looked at the book again. "Heat trick," he murmured. "It does sound easy. Though now that I think of it, I'm not sure I've ever actually seen a ryū egg, hatched or unhatched."

"Of course you haven't." Yuharu flicked her tail dismissively. "You've never been to Ryūgū-jō."

"*Ryūgū-jō?*"

Ryūgū-jō was a mythical place—a red-and-white coral palace in the darkest depths of the sea, the domain of the ancient ryū gods. It had disappeared so long ago that it was even more of a mystery than the giant ryū themselves. When Kohei was a baby, someone gave him a picture book with a full-color illustration of the palace— he remembered pressing his tiny fingertips against the elegant image, half believing that he'd be able to touch the magic itself if he tried hard enough.

"Not the *real* Ryūgū-jō," Yuharu said. "A newer one. It's a replacement of sorts—they built it near the coast, in Chiba, sometime after the war. It's where ryū eggs are collected and kept safe. We don't lay them like chickens, after all."

Cheshire nodded. "For us . . . Beit Lechem, and pilgrimage," he murmured. "The same."

Isolde seemed thrilled to hear Cheshire's voice, and she smiled at him encouragingly, but he fell silent—those few words had completely exhausted him.

Kohei considered all of this. He considered his father's inked notes in the margins of Dr. Arima's book, and the weight of the silver lighter in his pocket, and the way

Ojiisan had tried to sit up in his hospital bed. How he couldn't, because he was so weak. How angry he sounded, how tired.

He considered the cost of a train ticket to the New Ryūgū-jō.

It was the easiest decision he'd ever made.

Kohei stood. His legs were asleep from sitting on the floor so long, and he stumbled, sending Yuharu tumbling away with a squawk. Isolde rose too, grabbing Yuharu and handing her off to Kohei. "Are we done?" she asked. "Are you going to bed now? It must be almost sunrise."

"No," Kohei said.

Yamenaide. He would not stop.

"Ooooo-kay. Then what are you doing?"

He didn't answer. He strode to Papa's desk and rummaged around the clutter until he found it—his father's briefcase. It was empty, and had been for a very long time.

Yuharu nudged the side of his neck. "Answer her, Kohei," she said. "I wouldn't mind knowing, myself."

"Where are you *going?*" Isolde asked.

"Ōsaka-eki," said Kohei. "To catch a train."

"What, to Chiba? No, Kohei, you can't!" Isolde's voice was fierce. "Kohei, *stop.* Your mother was right; you need to be with your grandfather right now! You can't go off on some wild dragon-hatching quest. You need to spend time with your family before it's too late."

Kohei opened the briefcase and slipped Dr. Arima's book inside. He tried not to look at the small photograph that his father had tucked into the plaid lining—he knew that if he saw it, it would break him, and he would realize how tired he was. He would start crying.

It was a picture of him as a baby. Tiny little Kohei, with big, round eyes and a solemn frown.

Isolde took a step closer; her fierceness got quieter, but stronger all the same. "Kohei," she said, "do you know what Jewish people say instead of *rest in peace*? We say, 'zichronam l'vracha.' *May their memories be for a blessing.* Because so many of us have been killed—entire families, entire communities—and the only way we can make sense of it is by praying that their stories will have been for *good*, that their suffering might have changed things, and maybe . . ." She paused. "Kohei, are you listening to me? You have a chance to hear your grandfather's stories before it's too late! You have a chance to *remember* him, and you can't throw it away. You can't lose those stories—I won't let you!"

"I won't lose them," Kohei said simply. "Because I won't lose Ojiisan."

He could feel Isolde glaring at him—he couldn't bring himself to look, but he could imagine her tearful bitterness, her frustration. She thought he wasn't listening. But he *was*.

He knew that his grandfather's story hung in the balance. But Isolde had been there at the hospital—she'd seen what was left of him. Did she really think the old man would be willing to talk at a time like this?

If Ojiisan could tell his stories, he wouldn't drink so much. If Ojiisan could share his nightmares, he wouldn't spend entire nights staring at the kitchen wall instead of going to sleep. If Ojiisan could talk . . .

If Ojiisan could talk, he would be able to feel things again, even if those things hurt. Things that hurt were able to heal.

Numb anger never would.

If he had the time to explain all of this, Kohei would. He would make Isolde understand. But he didn't have time.

He closed his father's briefcase with a dull thunk; the brass fasteners clicked into place. Kohei took a deep breath. He straightened his spine.

Yamenaide.

Kohei had lied. He *did* remember that little, cloth-bound Russian book. Seeing it was like seeing a memory's shadow.

He remembered how it had looked in his father's hand.

It had seemed like such a secret thing. His father held it as if it might burn him—or like maybe it already had.

"Books carry ideas, son, and ideas are dangerous things. Otherwise, they wouldn't matter so much." Papa's eyes were dark and deep; his forehead creased as he knelt to see Kohei's face. "Ideas can break families. Even ours. And having the wrong book can be unsafe. But we have them anyway, don't we? We hold them close."

Kohei wanted this memory to be as vivid as his memory of the ryū parade. He wanted to hear Papa's voice and feel his closeness and see all of him, not just his eyes, not just the way he cradled that little book in his hand.

But it wasn't vivid. It was so faded and foggy, a small part of Kohei wondered if he'd imagined the entire thing.

7

For a Blessing

It took some convincing, but once Isolde and Cheshire had retreated to the Carters' apartment, Kohei finally got Yuharu to explain the purpose of the New Ryūgū-jō. "Eastern dragons, or ryū, are of air and sea, just as Western dragons are of fire and stone," she told him, settling on his bed and resting her chin on his pillow. "While some Western dragons, like Cheshire, hatch from cave rocks high in the mountains, Japanese ryū and Chinese lóng are hatched from rocks found in the darkest depths of the ocean."

"You hatch from *rocks?*" said Kohei. He opened his wardrobe and peered into it, frowning. He could have sworn he'd seen some money stashed near the mothballs when he was younger, but he doubted it was still there.

"Not the pebbles you kick around on the street,"

Yuharu said. "And they're not really *eggs*, so they don't exactly *hatch*. They're called kuroi-ōyatama: large spheres of dark igneous rock that can absorb ryū DNA. Ōyatama are unearthly. Some say they're made of the same material found in the very core of the planet."

"If they're from the core of the planet, they're the opposite of unearthly," Kohei said. "They're . . . *super*-earthly."

"Ha *ha*," Yuharu said flatly. "What are you looking for in there?"

"Money."

"You think you'll find money in your wardrobe?"

"Well, where else? Mama stashes stuff in furniture all the time, and I've already checked most of the other cabinets."

Yuharu rose with a groan and climbed up the bedpost, settling like a stern gargoyle just above Kohei's head. "Kohei," she said.

"What does Ryūgū-jō have to do with ocean rocks?"

"Everything. A long time ago, all Eastern dragons maintained ties to our ancestral oceans, so we swam down regularly to find our own ōyatama. But most of us live with humans now, and those humans have flocked to inland cities. Not that any place in Japan is very far inland," she added practically, "but our cousins in China, the ancient dynastic lóng families, have been migrating out of their Shanghai estates for years. Have I ever told you about my brother's

friend, the one who became a botanist in the steppes of Central—"

"So since you've gotten used to living on land, you can't find your own super-earthly rocks in the ocean," Kohei interrupted her, still rummaging through his clothes.

Yuharu sighed. "We *can*," she said. "But it's a hassle. It's hard to travel deep enough when you're so small. We're more buoyant than our ancestors, and some of us aren't accustomed to swimming long distances."

"So . . ."

"So a replica of the Old Ryūgū-jō was built on the coast. Some say that, once or twice a month, an ancient ocean spirit comes ashore with a dozen ōyatama in tow, and he trades them to the Ōya-Keepers at the New Ryūgū-jō in exchange for a handful of rohai leaves."

"Leaves?" Kohei repeated. "Why would an ancient ocean spirit want *leaves?*"

Yuharu shrugged. "I doubt the story is remotely true," she said. "It's probably a marketing scheme, given that the New Ryūgū-jō has become a bit of a spectacle in recent years. I'm guessing they pay fishing companies to hand over any kuroi-ōyatama they find."

"Oh," said Kohei. He couldn't help but feel a little let down; the idea of a plant-loving ocean spirit was ridiculous, but there was something oddly wonderful about it too.

Yuharu heard the note of disappointment in his voice,

and she reached down to pat his head. "It's all right," she said. "There might be a bit of truth to the tale. It would certainly explain why the Ōya-Keepers bother growing rohai plants on the grounds."

"Why wouldn't they? Are they ugly, or something?"

"They're poison."

"Oh," Kohei said again.

"Well, that's not entirely fair. Any plant is poisonous if you eat enough of it; rohai is just stronger than most. At the proper dosage, it can help land animals extract oxygen from water. But it's volatile. Each leaf has a different level of strength, and no one's been able to figure out why. Or how to measure it."

Kohei shivered. "Maybe an ancient ocean spirit would find that kind of thing tasty," he said.

"I doubt ocean spirits have taste buds."

Kohei let out a triumphant yell. "Found it!" he exclaimed, sitting back on his heels to inspect the bundle of yen notes clutched in his hands. They smelled like mothballs and yukata fabric—like Mama—and he felt a momentary qualm. Just because the money was in his room didn't mean it was *his*.

"Congratulations, you've committed petty larceny," Yuharu said, echoing his thoughts.

"It's for Ojiisan," Kohei murmured. "It's for my family."

"Right." Yuharu shook her head. "Look, Kohei, I know what you're thinking—but it wouldn't work anyway. You need two dragons to hatch an ōyatama, or it's less of an 'egg' and more of a very rare paperweight. You only have—"

Kohei jumped to his feet and snatched her from the bedpost before she could finish her sentence. "I have you," he said, "and we can get Cheshire."

"Oh yeah?" Yuharu muttered, digging her claws into his shirt. "Cheshire's not the one who'll be difficult to convince."

"Are you *kidding* me?" Isolde demanded. "After everything I literally *just* said to you? Put that briefcase down!"

She hadn't gotten any more sleep than Kohei had; the first light of dawn was beginning to peek through the window outside the Carters' apartment door, and Isolde was still in her school uniform, including her too-big hat. She had dark shadows under her eyes. Cheshire was perched on her shoulder, blinking blearily.

"I need to do this," Kohei insisted. "Please . . . you're not going to change my mind."

"No, but I'm not going to encourage your delusion either!" Isolde looked to Yuharu, raising one eyebrow. "I'm surprised *you* are."

"I'm less than a foot tall," Yuharu retorted. "When he was a baby, all I had to do was threaten to bite his nose and he'd quiet right down. Things have gotten harder since he learned to walk."

Kohei ignored them. "I can pay for the tickets," he said to Isolde, "and I promise, it'll be a good learning experience for you. You'll like the weather in Chiba, I think, and—and—" He broke off, unable to come up with any more made-up reasons.

"*Please*," he whispered. "I need your help."

Isolde faltered, her scowl softening into something more uncertain. "Kohei . . ." she said.

"We don't have much time—it's almost sunrise, and we need to leave before our families wake up, or they'll stop us."

"But—"

"It's a long train ride, but I'll bring snacks."

"We can't leave without telling our parents!" Isolde exclaimed. "They'll think we've been kidnapped!"

"If we tell them, they'll stop us. They won't understand. We can leave a note."

"I don't want to abandon Cheshire . . ."

"Oh, you won't have to! We need him to come along."

Isolde glanced at the half-asleep dragon swaying on her shoulder. "Really?" she said. "Why? You told me he's too small to help you with your . . ." She grimaced. "*Adventure.*"

"Yuharu says we'll need dragon scales," Kohei explained. "Two scales, from two different dragons. If Cheshire's willing to donate one of his . . ."

He waited for Isolde to tell him it was a bad idea, and that she wasn't going to get mixed up with a scheme like this, not if it could put Cheshire in any sort of danger. He waited for her to roll her eyes at him and slam her apartment door in his face.

But she didn't.

Something had changed.

Kohei saw it in her face—he wasn't sure what it was exactly, but it was like a switch had been flipped. She didn't look skeptical anymore. There was a sudden softness in her expression. Not a *gentle* sort of soft . . . just *different*.

"Okay," she said. "I'll come. I'll help."

Then she pointed at him, and her sharpness was back. "But you'd better bring a *lot* of snacks!"

The train zoomed past Kyōto, toward Nagoya, clattering through the windswept fields.

"What's your grandfather's name?" Isolde asked suddenly. She was slumped against the wall of the train compartment, arms crossed tight, eyes nearly closed against the foggy sun. "I never thought to ask."

"His name is Kyōsuke," Kohei said. "Fujiwara Kyōsuke."

"He's your mother's father, right?"

"Yeah."

"But, uh . . . isn't Fujiwara also *your* . . . ?"

Kohei could see the question forming on her lips—it was one he'd recited the answer to at least a dozen times. "I was given my mother's maiden name when my father died," he said. "Ojiisan insisted. I was born Arahata Kohei; my father was Arahata Denjirō."

"Oh." Isolde's eyes flickered open, and Kohei could tell she wanted to know more, though she had the sense not to press him any further.

Kohei sighed. "I don't know the whole story," he admitted. "I asked about it a few times when I was younger, but it always made Mama upset, and I couldn't expect to get a straight answer out of my grandfather any-way. All I know is, I'm not an Arahata anymore."

"But you remember being an Arahata?"

"Yes. Sort of. Kind of." Kohei closed his eyes, search-ing for the fragments of Papa's voice, and those images of the ryū parade. "I was little when Papa died. There was a typhoon—you call them *hurricanes* in America. It was a big storm, but it seemed like any other night to me. You know how little kids are—they only get scared when their parents get scared, and I think Mama thought things were ordinary too. But Papa . . ."

Kohei's brow creased. "He was calm," he said. "But it was a strange sort of calm. The kind of calm that—well, the kind of calm that only comes at the ends of things."

His father had been tense but settled. He had been full of energy but not jumpy. He'd moved with slow deliberation, arranging things on the mantelpiece over and over until he was satisfied they were in the right place.

"And he kissed my forehead, and he said—" Kohei swallowed, needing to get the words out before they choked him. "He said, 'Make it mean something.'"

And then, Arahata Denjirō had left home for the last time. And Mama had gotten a call from the hospital late that night, but for the life of him, Kohei couldn't remember what her face had looked like when she'd picked up the phone. He couldn't remember what she'd sounded like, or if she could believe the news, or—

When Kohei opened his eyes, Isolde was studying his face. "Make it mean something," she echoed softly. "Make my memory be for a blessing."

Kohei nodded, trying not to shatter into a million pieces.

The train stopped at Shizuoka, passed the mountains and the sea.

"How old were you?" Isolde asked. "When your father died, I mean."

"Three or so."

"Oh."

There was a pause.

"I'm lucky to have both my parents," Isolde murmured.

"But you don't have grandparents," Kohei said.

The corner of Isolde's mouth twitched. "Everyone has grandparents, Kohei," she reminded him. "I just never got to meet mine."

"Right. Sorry." Kohei looked at his hands. "I'm glad I have Ojiisan—I'm lucky that way."

"Maybe." Isolde sounded unconvinced, and Kohei hated that he understood why.

"Do you ever think about what you'd say if you could meet your grandparents?" he asked her.

Isolde shrugged. "My mother's parents, maybe," she said. "They could speak English—they lived in the United States longer than I did. My grandmother was born in Sacramento, which isn't far from San Francisco. We could've had an actual conversation together, if she'd lived. But . . ." Isolde faltered. "But, I dunno—she *died*. I've only ever known her as a dead person. So even if she were suddenly alive again, what on earth could I even *say?*"

"And your grandparents are all like that," Kohei said. "They're all . . ."

Dead.

Isolde looked away from him. "Camps," she said, answering his actual question. "They all died in camps,

far from home. My mother's parents in Tule Lake, in California, and my father's parents in Treblinka, in—in Poland." Her voice went hoarse. "So when I imagine talking to them, or—or *meeting* them, even in my head, it's always like—I mean, you know what it's like to talk to people who've survived things. My dad survived, and he *never*—"

She clamped her mouth shut, swallowing and blinking furiously.

Kohei waited.

A few deep breaths, and then Isolde attempted a smile. "I guess what I'm saying is," she said, "I wouldn't have blamed you if you *were* trying to run away from your grandfather's stories. Remembering hurts, and it feels unfair sometimes that we're the ones who have to keep doing it. But here we are."

The train pushed through Kanagawa Prefecture, up through Tōkyō and down again.

"What were their names?" Kohei asked.

Isolde knew what he meant, and she smiled for real. "My dad's parents were Chava and Chaskel Woźnica," she said, repeating the syllables carefully, like a prayer. "They changed Dad's last name when they sent him to America, which is why I'm Isolde Carter. It's easier to spell, I guess. And Mama's parents were John and Betty Sato."

"I wish they'd had a chance to meet you," Kohei said. "They would've been proud to know you, I think."

Color rose in Isolde's cheeks. "Thanks," she murmured. Then she looked up, and said in the most earnest voice Kohei had ever heard, "I'm glad your grandfather really *did* have a chance to know you. He's so lucky to have you."

Kohei wasn't sure that was true, but he thanked her anyway.

Isolde dozed off for a bit after that. Clearly, she was right—remembering was exhausting. But Kohei couldn't sleep. It was so quiet, the kind of quiet that can only exist on a train—a swaying, thrumming, constantly moving sort of quiet.

Cheshire was awake. He gazed out the window, watching the scenery pass with a thoughtful frown. Not for the first time, Kohei wondered what went on in the little Western dragon's head.

They were still a little awkward around each other. It was partly because they didn't have a common language between them, but, mostly, Kohei wasn't sure if Cheshire had forgiven him for all the yelling and insults. He wasn't sure if the little dragon had been angry in the first place.

What's more, Kohei wasn't sure if he *deserved* to be forgiven.

He needed Cheshire in order to hatch an ōyatama at New Ryūgū-jō, and Cheshire seemed perfectly willing

to play along, if only for Isolde's sake. The two had a different bond than Kohei and Yuharu did; it was deep, and quiet, and complicated.

So was Kohei's own relationship with Isolde, in a way. She'd said a bunch of times that they were friends—the kind of friends who were willing to visit each other's dying family members. Which was another thing Kohei wasn't sure he actually deserved.

Friendship. Weird, unconditional friendship.

Tadashi and Hisao had made their opinions on the subject *very* clear. And it wasn't that Kohei missed those old friends of his—in fact, he kind of hated them for the way they'd treated Isolde. What bothered him was the fact that he didn't know what had made them change. What had made them suddenly stop liking him.

What was it Hisao had said outside the ryū den that day? *My mother told me what your family's like.* Kohei wondered if Mrs. Abe would be willing to share that information. He'd been trying to get his family's history out of Mama and Ojiisan for years, to no avail.

He shook his head, trying to clear his mind. There was nothing he could do about his former friends. All he could do was try to deserve his new one. So when Isolde finally woke up, blinking groggily, he gathered all his courage and smiled at her—a real, shy smile. "I wanted to thank you," he began.

"Oh?" said Isolde. "For what?"

"For—" Kohei hesitated. "Well, for coming to Chiba with me. You're kind to me, and I'm not always sure why."

"Hm," Isolde said thoughtfully; apparently, that hadn't occurred to her before. "Well . . . if it helps, I'm not here *just* for you."

It actually did help. A lot.

Isolde sat up, seeming to consider her words carefully before saying them aloud. "I'm here for me, too," she said. "I didn't want to come at first, because there was a part of me that thought you were trying to hop on a train and never come back, and even though I understood it, I didn't want you to regret things the way I do. But you're not just running away. And when I heard your plan . . ."

She looked down at her hands, clasped together against her knees. "Kohei," she said, "tell me honestly . . . do you think I'll ever be able to speak Japanese?"

"Of course," said Kohei, startled by the sudden change in subject. "You'll get better at it. It just takes practice."

"Yeah, but—" Isolde faltered. "But will I ever sound like a native speaker? Like *you*."

Oh.

Kohei had to admit that that was a different question altogether. *A native speaker?* He knew he would never sound like an American, no matter how fluent he became

in English. It would never be his *first* language—Japanese was. But that didn't matter much to him, as long as people were able to . . .

. . . understand him.

"I don't think so," he said slowly. "Maybe. I don't know. Does that matter to you?"

Isolde shrugged, her cheeks turning pink.

Maybe talking about feelings was easier when the feelings weren't yours. Kohei waited awhile for Isolde to explain her question further, but she never did, and he wasn't sure how to ask her if she wanted to. After all, it felt a little hypocritical; he'd spent most of the past twenty-four hours refusing to talk himself.

Eventually, Isolde looked up at him. "Um," she said, then looked down again, hunching her shoulders. "I . . ."

He waited.

"Hazukashī," Isolde mumbled. *I'm embarrassed.* "Hana-sukoto ga sukidake—suki da kere—kedo . . . hanase—sa—nakereba . . . ike—*ikya* . . ."

I like to talk. I need to talk. If I don't talk . . .

Isolde was the sort of person who talked through her problems. For the first time, Kohei realized how awful she must feel, dropped in this place where, for the first time since she was a baby, she literally couldn't *speak*. It was probably the same way Kohei felt when he was faced with problems he didn't know how to fix: helpless. Trapped in his own head and frozen in place, watching everything move around him, wanting to tell it all to just *stop*.

Isolde gave up. "And you know the worst part?" she blurted out. "Here, I'm American—I'm the most American person a lot of people know. But do you know what I was in America?" She threw her hands up in frustration. "I was the most Japanese person anyone knew! So now it just feels like I'm cheating."

"Cheating at what?"

"At—at *being*! At existing! I was a fake Japanese person in America, and here, I'm a fake American."

"Fake . . . American," Kohei echoed, wondering if something important had just been lost in translation.

"I feel like I'm—oh, what's the word in Japanese?" She frowned. "Is it *dasu*? Dashita . . . dashimasu?"

"That means *to take out*," Kohei said.

"Ugh, never *mind*." Isolde buried her head in her hands.

Yuharu, who'd woken up in time to hear most of their conversation, cleared her throat. "The dragon we're going to hatch," she said. "It's not just going to be big. It's also going to be half-Western, half-Eastern, like you. Is that what you're trying to say?"

Isolde shook her head. "It won't be half *anything*," she said, her voice muffled. "*I'm* not half anything. I'm not divided into parts, I'm just *me*: one single person that's a

bunch of things all at once. And a mixed dragon would be like that, too. The two of us could be lots of things *together*, and neither one of us would have to pick a side."

"Pick a side," Kohei echoed. He felt a bit lost. Maybe he needed to review some of these English words.

Isolde huffed and turned to the window, staring at the landscapes skipping past. "Maybe . . . maybe it's different in Japan," she said. "But in America, race is everything. For some people, it's all they understand—it's the only thing they care about. And I don't fit. I can't be *both*—I have to be *either*, which sort of means I'm *neither*. Does that make sense? People don't know whether or not they're supposed to hate me—if I'm part of *us* or part of *them*. Like, even though there's no war anymore, everyone still wants to tell me which part of myself I'm allowed to be."

That made sense in a way—it was like when Kohei was changed from an Arahata to a Fujiwara. He was still both, but he couldn't be *called* both.

And unlike his name, Isolde's bothness was written across her face and woven into her hair.

"If it makes you feel any better," Kohei said, "I'm really glad you're you."

Isolde gave him a small smile. Cheshire let out a soft, thrumming noise and crawled onto her lap, nudging her elbow with his snout—*me too*, he seemed to say. And

Kohei realized that Cheshire understood bothness too. He spoke Yiddish, which was an entire language of *both*.

Isolde's smile faded, and she stroked the top of Cheshire's head with her finger. "It will be different when there are mixed dragons too," she said. "I know it will. It's simpler for people to understand things when it's not their own prejudices at stake." She looked at Kohei pleadingly. "Right?"

Kohei nodded. "Maybe," he murmured.

To his surprise, Isolde wasn't disappointed that he hadn't said *yes* outright. "Maybe," she repeated, sitting back in her seat. The flush began to fade from her cheeks. "Maybe is enough."

Tails thick enough to crush a whole apartment building. Talons against old asphalt . . . long, coiled bodies . . . glimmering fur. And the Western dragon circling overhead, protecting everybody. Flying.

Soaring.

As the train pulled into the station at Chiba, Kohei went through every detail of his impossible memory, holding every piece of it, trying to memorize each one. Some of them seemed shabbier than usual—the closer he looked, the odder certain things seemed:

The weather was cold and hot all at once.

The sky was bright but the eyes of the ryū were shadowed.

The buildings were lopsided.

Kohei puzzled over these mismatched things, but dismissed them before they could bother him too much. This memory was *his*—it was the place he retreated to when he had nowhere else to go.

He couldn't break it. Not now.

8
Easy-Peasy

"So, this *is the New Ryūgū-jō?*" Isolde said skeptically. "It kinda looks like a mini version of Disneyland."

Kohei had never been to Disneyland, but he had to admit he wasn't impressed with the New Ryūgū-jō either. It didn't look anything like an ancient shrine—more like an amusement park. The front gates were made of faded, peeling wood, and he could see small carnival rides inside, supervised by teens in mascot costumes, their bored-looking little ryū chewing up used tickets. It was nothing like the Old Ryūgū-jō, the underwater palace of red and white coral. This place was clearly built by humans. And it was *really* showing its age.

It was warm out, and the place was buzzing with activity. There were lots of young kids on the rides, and

their parents milled about, peering at the ryū statues positioned in strategic spots around the grounds. The statues looked impressive from a distance, but when Kohei got closer, he saw that they weren't even ryū; they were plaster versions of the Chinese lóng statues from the Forbidden City in Beijing. Everything here was a replica of the wrong thing. Kohei knew better than to be disappointed . . .

But when it comes to disappointment, *knowing* better rarely makes any difference.

Since this was a tourist attraction, there were faded posters plastered all over the place, most featuring smiley cartoon ryū, all heavily graffitied. Kohei went up to the sign that showed a ryū with sunglasses spray-painted atop its snout. *Ōya-Keepers have been employed at the New Ryūgū-jō since 1946*, the caption read. *Fun fact: Some of them are licensed to breed ryū in more than one country!*

"Very helpful," Kohei muttered.

He shifted his attention to Isolde, who had drifted over to a different poster. It looked newer than the others; it wasn't as faded, and there were French, English, and Korean translations printed beneath the original Japanese.

"What does it say?" Kohei asked, jogging to catch up with her.

" 'New Ryūgū-jō also contains the world's finest rohai gardens.' " Isolde frowned. "Rohai? What's rohai?"

"Poison," Yuharu said. She was sitting stiff as a rod on Kohei's shoulder, her arms folded and her brows drawn into a scowl. She'd been on edge since they'd walked through the gates of this paper-thin replica of her ancestral home. Cheshire, on the other hand, looked amused by all the carnival music.

"Poison?" Isolde's eyes widened. "Why would anyone grow *poison* at an amusement park? I mean, Disney doesn't sell Snow White's apples in their theme parks, do they?"

That was a good point. Unfortunately, after a few minutes of searching, they couldn't find a single poster with any sort of explanation. Rohai plants were never mentioned again, unless you counted the *DANGER* signs posted just outside the garden.

Isolde shied away from the small, leafy plants when she saw those red-and-yellow signs. She may not have known Japanese very well, but warning symbols were scary in any language. Yuharu tried to get Kohei to keep his distance too—she dug her talons into his ear and tugged as if she were trying to pull back the reins on a disobedient horse. But he ignored her.

There was something strange about these plants.

Not *dangerous* strange. Not safe strange either, but—well, Kohei could have sworn he knew them. *Understood* them. Like in the mornings sometimes, when he caught the scent of shaving cream in the hall outside his bedroom and knew

that Ojiisan must've walked past. It was like hearing Papa's voice in his head without really remembering . . .

"Kohei!" Yuharu hissed, yanking his earlobe hard enough to draw blood. "What are you *doing?*"

He was moving closer to the rohai patch. That's what he was doing.

And he was kneeling at the edge, his knees sinking into the dirt.

And he was—

"Don't touch that," Yuharu snapped. "Kohei, that's—"

But Kohei couldn't hear her anymore. There was something familiar about the rounded edges of the rohai leaves. Kohei lifted one with the tip of his finger. It was like recognizing a stranger. Something about these rohai plants reminded him of something . . . memories long forgotten. A memory he was supposed to have.

How could something like this be *poison?*

Kohei didn't know why he plucked a half-dried rohai stalk from the edge of the garden. He didn't know why he tucked it furtively into his pocket, glancing around to make sure no grown-ups saw.

He didn't know. But whatever the reason was, it didn't seem important—he just knew it was *right*. So Kohei ignored Yuharu's irritated scolding and jogged to rejoin Isolde, the bundle of leafy secrets safely in one pocket, Papa's lighter in the other.

As cluttered and disorganized as most of the amusement park was, the Egg Pavilion itself was easy enough to find. It stood out—a large, white, smooth, oblong shape, more *egg* than *pavilion*. It had no doors, just a dark archway leading someplace cool and quiet. Kohei, Yuharu, Cheshire, and Isolde lingered outside, all suddenly overcome with uncertainty. There was something otherworldly about this place. Compared to the bustling, carefree laziness of the rest of New Ryūgū-jō, this place seemed completely still and completely solemn, as if they were standing at the edge of an iceberg, staring into a vast, shadowy abyss.

"Are we allowed to go inside?" Isolde whispered. There wasn't a real reason for her to lower her voice, but somehow they all knew: this was a whispering kind of place.

"I don't see why not," said Yuharu.

"But nobody else is. There's no line or anything."

"If you came to ride a roller coaster, would you bother stopping at a shrine?"

Fair point.

Kohei gave Isolde a reassuring nod before tiptoeing inside. Once they were through the entryway, they saw that it wasn't completely dark in the Pavilion—but it was very cold. Isolde shivered as she drew up beside him.

There were no super-earthly rocks, as far as Kohei could see. The Pavilion was a vast, circular space, all wood

and tatami and strings of paper-lantern lights. The floor was hard and smooth, but it also looked woven, like a rattan basket; when Kohei took a few tentative steps, the thump of his sneakers echoed, but nothing creaked.

It was so quiet. The kind of quiet that made the outside world seem like a half-remembered childhood. Kohei swallowed hard. "Sumimasen?" he called. "Ojamashimasu."

At first, there was no response. But then—

"Dōshitan desu ka?" A middle-aged man with tousled salt-and-pepper hair shuffled toward the center of the room. He was dressed all in white and looked startled, like he'd just woken up. His eyes widened when he saw Kohei and Isolde and their two dragons. "Eh?" he said.

"Excuse me, sir," Isolde said politely, in English. "We'd like a dragon egg, if possible."

Kohei opened his mouth to translate for her, but the Ōya-Keeper replied—also in English—before he had a chance. "Dragon egg?" he said, narrowing his eyes. "You can purchase them at the gift shop. Two hundred yen each, though if you buy a full set—"

"A real one," said Kohei. "Do you have them?"

The Ōya-Keeper blinked a few times. "Oh?" he said. "A real one? Hmph." He glanced at Yuharu and Cheshire. "Why?"

"To hatch," Yuharu said patiently.

"Oh. Right. Sure." The Ōya-Keeper scrutinized them

for a moment. "How old are all of you? Where are your parents?"

"Ch-chikaku ni," Isolde stammered. "That means 'nearby' in Japanese, right? Sorry, I haven't learned much of the language yet."

Kohei tried not to smile. Isolde was a terrible liar, but she also wasn't a good Japanese speaker, and the Ōya-Keeper would never know the difference.

What a clever friend he had.

The Ōya-Keeper gave them one last, long look, then rubbed his brow in tired resignation. "We do have some eggs," he said. "There are some left over after every migration, and we can't exactly throw them away, can we?"

Kohei's heart began to beat harder, fast enough that he worried it might jump up into his throat. "You have some?" he said. "Where are they? Can we have one? We'll be careful, we promise!"

Yuharu snorted. "Way to play it cool, buddy," she muttered.

The Ōya-Keeper shrugged one shoulder. "*Careful* has nothing to do with it," he said. "The eggs are basically rocks—very difficult to break. It's just that we've had a few people try to sell them on the black market. You know . . . the *illegal* one."

"We won't do that," Isolde assured him.

"You won't?" The Ōya-Keeper squinted at her, but

shook his head before she could answer. "No, you know what? It's better if I don't know. I don't get paid enough during the off-season to care. That said . . ." He paused meaningfully. "I *do* work for tips."

Isolde sighed, then glanced at Kohei.

He nodded.

"A thousand yen?" she offered.

"Done. Much obliged." The Ōya-Keeper took his money, counted it, then tipped his head toward a heavy curtain on one side of the pavilion. "The tama are all back there—knock yourselves out. If you're up to some sort of mischief, though, don't tell anyone I saw you."

He shuffled away.

The curtained-off doorway led to a narrow hallway, which led to a low-ceilinged chamber at the back of the Egg Pavilion. It was even darker than the Pavilion itself and had a packed-dirt floor. In the center of the room, Kohei spotted a small, jade bowl. And then he saw them: a half-dozen dragon eggs, nestled on a tatami mat in the corner. Cheshire and Yuharu went over to pick one while Kohei and Isolde knelt down beside them to watch.

Apparently, there was a whole process for it: Yuharu tilted her head by each of the rough egg-stones, listening for something that Kohei couldn't hear. Cheshire hovered behind her, a little more uncertain. Every once in a while, Yuharu gestured toward one of the stones, asking for his opinion. This wasn't his ancestral home, but he was still a dragon, and he could hear the ōyatama's music too.

"Kohei?" Yuharu called, tapping a particularly ordinary-looking rock. "If you'd like to make yourself useful, bring this one to the jade bowl, please."

Ordinary-looking or not, the ōyatama was larger than Kohei thought it would be, and heavier too. He grimaced as he set it in place. "Are they all this dense?" he asked.

"No," Yuharu replied. She was much less grumpy now that the merry-go-rounds were out of sight. "Each ōyatama has its own nature, its own personality. This one is settled and down-to-earth, like me. It told me so."

"Right," said Kohei, half-convinced she was teasing him. "So, what do we do?"

"Do you see the ridges on the sides of the egg? There should be one that's deeper than the others. That's the spot where the egg can absorb DNA from the scales."

"It's that easy?" Isolde asked.

"Yep. As you Americans would say, 'easy-peasy-lemon-squeezy.'"

"Lemon *what?*"

Kohei was too focused on their mission to laugh at Isolde's indignation. Mostly, he was focused on the small,

smooth weight in his pocket: Papa's silver cigarette lighter, cold and heavy as a stone. Removing it from Papa's study had felt odd, but there was something poetic about using it here. Kohei knew from their study session that if he applied heat at the right time, the dragon would have "big" DNA, and Ojiisan might look at it like he did in the impossible memory of the ryū parade, and then, *maybe*, everyone in his family could be happy again. Like Papa would've wanted.

"All right," Kohei said, trying to hide the tremor in his voice. "Let's do this."

He thought that pulling a scale would be painful for Yuharu and Cheshire, but, to his surprise, they each plucked one off of their spines without flinching. It was like picking a loose hair from a human's head. They also didn't seem to care that they were about to pass on their DNA to a brand-new, living creature—it barely seemed to matter to them. It seemed strange to Kohei, human as he was, but he was too fascinated to ask questions. Yuharu saw him staring and handed him her pink scale so he could have a closer look. Cheshire gave his reddish one to Isolde.

Isolde peered at the tiny, perfect shard in the palm of her hand. "Wow," she said, awestruck. "I never realized they were so pretty on their own. It looks like broken pottery, but . . . deeper."

"Yours is almost glittering, Yuharu," Kohei remarked,

pressing it between his fingers. It was light but sturdy, like a gemstone.

"That's water magic," Yuharu said. "Chiba is near the ocean—my scales wouldn't look the same if we were farther inland, and Cheshire's would likely look different in the mountains, or on the Siberian plateau."

"There's really magic here?" Isolde whispered.

"I'll bet there's even more of it in the Old Ryūgū-jō," said Kohei.

Yuharu nodded. "That's what my father always said," she murmured. "Though it was difficult, with him, to determine what was a memory and what was fiction."

Isolde stared at Cheshire's scale one second longer before handing it back to him. It didn't look as luminous as Yuharu's—he had no ties to the ocean or the sky. But it was still beautiful, in a simple, quiet way. Beautiful like clay, like earth.

Cheshire pressed his scale against the surface of the ōyatama. Yuharu nodded approvingly. "See how it's melting a little bit?" she said. "It's fusing to the egg. But it can't do much until another scale is introduced. It's our turn, Kohei."

Kohei swallowed. *No turning back.*

He handed the scale back to Yuharu, then shifted closer so he could see her insert it into the deep ridge on the egg's surface. Her scale dissolved faster than Cheshire's had—it truly was melting into the egg, merging the heat

of dragon histories with the coldness of deep-sea stone. Kohei's heart fluttered—*this was it*. This was real. They were making history.

For Ojiisan.

For Isolde.

Before long, a deep glow began to pulse within the previously icy stone egg; its power prickled across Kohei's skin, and he shifted back on his heels, nervous. "It's not going to explode, is it?" he asked.

"No," Yuharu said. "The outer shell will crack before the pressure inside becomes too great."

"Are you sure? Like, *really* sure?"

He didn't get a response. Yuharu looked like she was falling into a trance; the egg's inner light was reflected in her clear, dark eyes. Cheshire shifted closer to her, equally hypnotized. Isolde glanced at Kohei, then looked down again. It *was* a truly beautiful sight. The egg's power surged back and forth, brighter and brighter—the energy wasn't in the shell itself but in the fluid held in its core. It looked like the rock was melting into magma—or ocean water. As it glowed with more and more intensity, Kohei could've sworn he saw the dragon forming inside. He made out its silhouette, growing and shifting and squirming.

It was already so lovely. He didn't want to do anything to change it.

Except.

Except Papa's engraved cigarette lighter was like a lead padlock in his pocket, a weight he couldn't ignore. He drew it out with one hand, flicked the lever until a flame snapped up, and held it near the base of the rock. The wavering light illuminated the stone's roughness, darkening it, scorching it, until its surface settled, now as smooth as polished obsidian.

Kohei drew back, his heart thumping in his chest like a drum.

The small chamber felt like the inside of a tea kettle before long—it wasn't that hot, but Kohei could hear the sort of high-pitched, shrieking sound that made him think the egg was going to explode and kill them all. Yuharu hadn't actually *said* they were safe, had she?

No, she definitely hadn't!

But just as Kohei started calculating the likelihood of being blinded by egg shrapnel, there was a loud, cracking noise, and the rock split into two jagged halves. There, curled in its stony cradle, was a tiny, brand-new dragon, pulsing with life.

It was the most beautiful thing Kohei had ever seen.

9
Mukashi Banashi

"It's so cute," Isolde whispered.

"It's so *colorful.*" Kohei leaned a little closer to get a better look. The dragon smelled like cotton blankets and a candle burning low. It wasn't pink like Yuharu, or any other color Kohei had seen on a dragon. Its scales were a beautiful, darkish gold. Its legs were like Cheshire's, but it had tufts of fur like Yuharu. The fur wasn't white; it looked more like mist, or a rainstorm so thick, you could reach out and grab the water with your hand.

The dragon cracked one eye open, and Kohei gasped. Its irises were a deep, plum color, with scattered shards of indigo and goldenrod, and its soft, dark pupil seemed to swell as it focused on Kohei's face.

"Hello, little guy," Isolde whispered.

"It's not a guy," said Yuharu.

"Really?"

"Of course not. Can't you tell?" Yuharu rolled her eyes at Isolde's foolishness and clambered down Kohei's arm to speak to the little hatchling. "Yōkoso," she welcomed it, beaming. "Aren't you a beautiful little thing?"

The newborn dragon seemed to brighten at the compliment, even though Kohei doubted it understood any words yet. It stretched its scrawny little legs and extended its wings—they were almost translucent, with the rainbow sheen of a dark opal. Isolde gasped. "So delicate," she whispered.

Kohei knew what she meant. The baby's wings were paper-thin and seemed like they'd tear if someone looked at them too hard. But even more astonishing was their enormous size. Each individual wing was nearly as long and as broad as Kohei's hand. Kohei had seen photographs of newly hatched Japanese ryū with their sturdy, thumb-length little wings; they weren't at all fragile, but they also didn't grow much once the ryū had hatched. This new dragon was delicate, but that delicacy also had the promise of strength and growth. She looked like a butterfly that had just emerged from its chrysalis. Kohei had a feeling that, one day, she would be able to fly like the Western dragon in his impossible memory.

All he had to do was protect her until she was strong enough to make her own way in the world, keep her safe and warm and loved, and someday she would live among the clouds.

It was amazing. Kohei had not anticipated how much he would love this beautiful creature.

"What's her name?" he asked aloud.

Yuharu shrugged. "Dragons aren't born with names," she said.

"Who named you?"

"Your father." Yuharu held Kohei's solemn gaze. "'Kohei and Yuharu,' he said—'partners in crime.'"

Isolde smothered a giggle. "I think I would've liked your dad, Kohei," she said.

"Me too," Kohei said. He looked down at the new dragon again. She was starting to explore the remaining fragments of her egg, poking the dirt below with her teeny claws. "Isolde, do you want to name her?"

"Me?" said Isolde. "Are you sure?"

"Yeah. Who else?"

Isolde stared at him, wide-eyed. She looked down at the new dragon, then up at Kohei, then down again, and then at Cheshire.

Cheshire reached out to touch her cheek with one paw. He murmured something gentle, something too quiet for Kohei to hear—*probably something encouraging*, Kohei thought. Or maybe just Isolde's name.

Isolde blinked rapidly, nodded, then offered her hand to the new dragon. "She ought to have a name that's both Western and Eastern," she said, smiling as the baby clamped its talons around her finger. "Do those exist?"

"There are a few," Kohei said. "I once knew a kid named Noa. I think that's a name in America, isn't it?"

Isolde wrinkled her nose. "There was a boy named Noah in my Hebrew school class in New York," she said. "He was the worst. Any other ideas?"

"Hana," Yuharu suggested. "That's what Kohei's mother's ryū is called. It's similar to Hannah."

"We can't have two dragons with the same name!" Kohei exclaimed.

Yuharu gave him a narrow look. "*Well*," she said. "If you have any better ideas, now would be the time to let us know."

"I do, actually," Kohei said. He tried very hard not to look smug; it definitely didn't work. "Naomi."

"Naomi?" said Isolde. She said it differently, of course—like *Neigh-oh-mee* instead of *Nah-o-mi.* "I like that name. I think it's Hebrew too."

A name—a new name. A perfect name. Kohei grinned. "Naomi," he said. He touched the top of the little

dragon's head, and she squinted at him the way dogs do when they're pleased. "Do you like your name, Naomi?"

Naomi let out a throaty, cooing noise. Yes, she liked it very much. Even though she'd literally just been born, she already had her own personality—social, like Yuharu, but much more cheerful. She wagged her long, spiky tail like a puppy, which made Isolde laugh, which made *Naomi* laugh and wag her tail again and again, just for giggles.

Kohei wasn't one to giggle, but even *he* couldn't keep from smiling. And it wasn't just because he was amused. It was because he could see both Naomi's Westernness and her bigness. She was small enough to climb up a kid's arm, but still noticeably bigger than Yuharu and Cheshire—her paws were *huge*, almost the size of Kohei's palm. Yuharu's were only the size of coins, and Cheshire's even smaller than that.

Papa had loved dogs, and whenever they walked past a puppy on the street, he'd always remark on the size of its paws. *There is a dog called a Great Dane,* he'd once told Kohei. *They often only weigh a few dozen grams at birth, but they can grow up to ninety kilos! You can never predict how big any creature will grow, Kohei-kun . . . but the paws are often a good hint.*

Naomi was going to grow into something great. Kohei *knew* it. Her eyes, now fully open, were even bigger than human eyes. She'd *have* to grow into them someday. She might not get as big as the ryū in Kohei's impossible memory, but after a few generations had passed . . . well, maybe her descendants would be.

Maybe.

And *maybe* was enough for now. More than enough! It had been so long since Kohei had been able to believe in a *maybe*.

He pulled Papa's lighter from his pocket once again, weighing it in his palm and rubbing the smooth metal with his thumb. The worn engraving—*kega, hurt*—felt the same as it always had, but it was also different somehow, heavier. Like Papa was trying to say something through the words he'd once carried in his own pocket. Kohei couldn't hear that deep, low voice—his father wasn't there, but he wanted to be. He was trying to be.

What did Papa need to say?

Kohei was still listening for Papa's voice when he heard soft, heavy footsteps behind him. He wouldn't have heard them if he hadn't been listening carefully; maybe that was why an uneasy chill pricked its way down his spine.

Isolde and Cheshire, who were facing the door, saw the intruder before he did. Their stricken expressions, half awe and half terror, told Kohei all he needed to know.

Someone, or something, was behind him. Something powerful, and maybe old. Something not quite human, something—

Kohei turned around.

It wasn't a big ryū like the ones Kohei had dreamed of, but it was certainly a bigg*er* ryū. It definitely wasn't a bored teenager in a mascot costume. Even from across the enclosure of the shadowed sanctuary, Kohei could make out the brilliant, inhuman eyes that marked this creature as a ryū through and through.

Not as big as a building. But certainly bigger than Kohei. It was actually around Ojiisan's size, but the thick layers of slatelike scales must have made it twice as heavy. They certainly made it twice as imposing.

This was a water ryū of some sort, but not the truly enormous kind. Not like the ones in Kohei's impossible memory. Those had been long and muscled, like serpents made of wind and clouds. This ryū had a long body and probing whiskers that moved like they were underwater, but it didn't seem long or thin enough to coil like a snake. It was balanced on its hind legs, standing upright like a human. Kohei stared at it—what *was* it? Why was it *here?*

The strangest thing was, even its eyes looked more

human than the blank, gaping gaze of the truly giant ryū. This ryū looked canny and intelligent—and calculating.

Like Yuharu. A larger, more robust, darker, and stranger version of Yuharu.

And it was old. Very old.

Kohei gulped and stuffed his father's lighter into his pocket. "Yoroshiku onegai itashimasu," he said to the creature. His voice sounded smaller than usual; even the most formal of greetings didn't feel formal enough. The ryū gazed at him, imperious and silent.

Isolde drew up to his side like she was ready for a fight. "Kohei . . ." she whispered.

The big ryū's gaze instantly dropped and focused on Naomi, curled in Isolde's palms. "Dare ka?" he rumbled. *Who is this?*

The gentleness of the old ryū's deep, resonant voice made Kohei want to run and hide. Nothing was scarier than the kind of power that kept itself quiet. It reminded Kohei of the way Ojiisan spoke: a single word, casually dropped, leaving silence and devastation in its wake.

Isolde glanced at Kohei, then steeled herself. "Dare ka . . . *you?*" she retorted. "Dōyatte . . . *here?*"

The big ryū didn't even look at her. He simply took one slow step forward, then another, fixated on Naomi.

Kohei shifted his stance so that he could jump in front of Naomi to protect her if he needed to. "Who are you?"

he said in Japanese, translating Isolde's half-formulated questions. "How did you come to this place?"

They didn't get a response at first, but when the big ryū halted right in front of them, he glanced at Kohei and said, "Mukashi kara."

"Is that your name?" Isolde asked.

Kohei opened his mouth to translate her question— and answer it—but the big ryū beat him to it. "It is what I am," he said in English.

"Oh," said Isolde.

"'Mukashi' means *a long time ago*," Kohei told her in a low voice. "Like, *once upon a time*. So he's . . ."

"Oh!" Isolde repeated, in a different tone. "Well, that's very mysterious of you, Mr. Large Ryū. But if I might ask, *why* are you here? And why are you here *now?*"

For some reason, the big ryū's theatrical way of speaking seemed to have made her *less* afraid. Kohei couldn't say the same for himself. He slipped a trembling hand into his jacket pocket to squeeze his papa's lighter—*yamenaide, Kohei-kun.*

The big ryū frowned at Isolde. Like most ryū, his expressions mostly involved his bushy eyebrows drawing together. He looked quite formidable, but Isolde wasn't fazed. "You're not here to hurt us," she said. "You wouldn't need to act so dramatic to do that. But you're definitely trying to scare us. Is that why you're here? To scare us out of doing something? You've been staring at Naomi a lot."

The big ryū blinked at her. His eyes narrowed like he had to do some recalculating. Kohei glanced at Isolde in the meantime, shocked that she'd been so direct, but when he saw the tightness of fear on her face, he realized what she was doing. She was thinking aloud, reasoning through their current situation by talking through it. She could do that here because the big ryū spoke and understood English.

For the first time, Kohei caught a glimpse of how fierce Isolde must have been when she lived in the United States.

The big ryū opened his mouth, then closed it, then opened it again, then sighed. "Give me the little one," he said.

"Why?" Isolde demanded, tightening her grip.

"I will give her back. I promise." The big ryū— Kohei couldn't help but think of him as Mukashi, even though that obviously wasn't his real name—raised one bushy eyebrow. "Do you trust me?"

Kohei *did* trust him. But only in the way he trusted Ojiisan, which was never quite enough.

Still, they didn't have many alternatives, and Isolde knew it. She extended Naomi to him, and the little ryū-dragon hopped into Mukashi's much larger paw.

"What are you going to do?" Kohei blurted out. He couldn't help himself. "Are you some sort of doctor?"

Mukashi didn't answer. Honestly, Kohei hadn't expected him to. He watched, helpless, as the big, ancient ryū held Naomi up, inspecting her eyes, gently lifting one of her paws with a single, giant talon.

"Half-Eastern, half-Western," he mused aloud. "Interesting. I have not seen that before."

"Is that a problem?" Isolde asked. She tried valiantly to keep her voice steady, but Kohei could see that her lower lip was trembling.

"Eh? No, of course not." Mukashi shook his head. His whiskers wavered slowly, unnervingly, framing his face like wisps of smoke. "But there is still a wrongness about her, I'm afraid."

Isolde drew a sharp breath, but Kohei interrupted her before she had a chance to tell Mukashi that *he* was the one with a wrongness. "We don't know what you mean," he said. He said it in Japanese, hoping that Mukashi would answer that way too. He felt a twinge of guilt for purposefully excluding Isolde, but he had a feeling that, whatever the old ryū was about to say, it would be better if Isolde heard it from a friend.

Mukashi gave him a dark look. "You used the heat trick, didn't you?" he replied in Japanese.

Kohei's hand tightened around Papa's lighter. "Heat . . . trick?" he said, feigning ignorance.

Mukashi sighed—not in a frustrated way but a

disappointed one. "I don't see any matches," he said. "Did you use a lighter?"

"No!" Kohei said a little too quickly.

Isolde knew the Japanese word for *no*. "What did he ask?" she whispered. "What's wrong?"

Mukashi gave Kohei a withering look. Then he took in a deep, husky breath through his nostrils and exhaled through his mouth, enveloping Naomi almost completely in a wispy cloud—the breath was ashy gray like smoke, yet thin as steam. The entire room felt colder, like it had been winter this whole time but Kohei was only noticing it now.

Naomi inhaled part of the cloud. In a moment of irrational panic, Kohei wondered if Mukashi's coldness was poison—the big ryū had promised to give Naomi back in the end, but he'd never guaranteed that she would be alive.

But it wasn't poison. When Naomi emerged, she didn't look sick. Only startled. She blinked a few times, coughing.

Isolde lunged forward and snatched Naomi from Mukashi's grip. "What did you do to her?" she cried. "She's so cold!"

"She'll be fine now. Healthier. Dragon DNA is not meant to be manipulated—certainly not by humans." Mukashi turned toward Kohei again, his gaze colder than any ryū's breath. "How did you learn about the fire trick?" he asked.

"Did you reverse it?" asked Kohei.

"Tell me, boy."

Kohei's cheeks flushed with heat. He *was* a boy, and he knew that this ancient creature had every right to talk down to him, but that didn't mean the veiled insult didn't sting. "I read it in a book," he said.

"Which book?"

"Does it matter?"

Mukashi scrutinized Kohei's expression. The intense attention only made Kohei's skin feel hotter, prickly with sweat; the reasonable part of his brain began to extract itself from the rest of him. *Well,* it said, shrugging, *you're on your own now, buddy.*

"Did you use matches?" Mukashi asked.

"Does it *matter?*"

"Everything matters, especially when it comes to fire. Tell me."

Kohei felt a familiar, rising flush of anger in his throat. He swallowed. "I did not use matches," he said. "I used a cigarette lighter." He fumbled in his pocket—he wasn't sure why he thought he needed to prove he was telling the truth, but he had a feeling that Mukashi wouldn't believe him if he said the ocean was wet. He brandished the lighter like a badge of honor.

"Good." Mukashi glanced at the little thing as though he expected to be completely unimpressed by it.

But something changed when his eyes landed on those kanji.

怪我

Something shifted.

Something big.

Kohei wasn't sure he'd ever be able to explain what it was exactly that tipped out of balance right then. But it happened, and it happened because Mukashi recognized Papa's lighter.

The big ryū hadn't tried to look indifferent about anything until now. His disdain for Kohei, his interest in Naomi, his strange compassion for Isolde—they all showed on his weathered face. But at the sight of Papa's lighter, everything went blank—it was like a mask had dropped over Mukashi's face, and whatever it was hiding, it was something powerful and difficult to ignore.

Rage? Sadness? Loneliness? Joy?

Why?

"Where did you get that?" Mukashi asked in that low, terribly gentle voice.

"What do you mean?"

"Did you find it somewhere?" The big ryū stalked forward before Kohei could react and plucked the lighter

right out of his hand, gazing at it like it was a precious, beautiful, tragically rare stone.

"It's mine!" Kohei cried. It was the most important thing he had, and yet for some reason, he couldn't bring himself to lunge for it. "Give it back!"

"Where was it? In the rubble somewhere?" Mukashi frowned in an abstract sort of way. He wasn't even looking at Kohei or Isolde—it was like they weren't there. "It should not have been discarded. It never should have been . . ."

Kohei's hands balled into sweaty fists, and he gritted his teeth, but it was like he was frozen in place—maybe out of anger, or maybe out of fear. He felt like he was edging across a tightrope wire, barely keeping his balance—if this awful ryū took away something of Papa's, he would fall. His entire life would be divided into two halves: before he met Mukashi, and after. And he couldn't bear that.

"Give. It. Back," he said, in English, with as much fury as he could muster. Still, his voice trembled.

Mukashi still had that distant look in his eyes, like he was seeing something he'd forgotten he was supposed to remember. Something from a very long time ago. "Take Naomi home," he murmured, turning to leave. With Papa's lighter still clasped between his talons. "I regulated her body temperature—she will be oddly proportioned for the rest of her life, but she will be healthy otherwise."

Kohei opened his mouth to bellow something, anything, that would make him seem like an actual threat.
He didn't have talons. He didn't have armor. He didn't
have fire. What did he have? What did he have left?

No words came out. It was like the terror and fury
had overheated him, and his brain was shutting down
until he could cool off. But there was no time to cool
off, because—

Because the big ryū, who'd never even told them his
real name, had already turned and ducked through the
heavy curtains that separated the small hatching chamber
from the rest of the Egg Pavilion. He was gone.

10
From New to Old

The heat disappeared far too quickly. Kohei was left standing there, empty-handed, with the same cold, hollow-bone feeling he'd had at the hospital, after Isolde had dragged him out of Ojiisan's room. But this time, it was worse. Isolde, Naomi, Cheshire, and Yuharu were with him, but he still felt all alone.

He'd lost Papa's favorite lighter.

No—it had been stolen from him.

It took Kohei a moment to remember where he was. That he was in a small room, not a big, infinite chasm. That he was standing upright, not sprawled flat on his back. But then he did remember. And he knew what he had to do.

He launched himself through the silk curtains, not even bothering to pick Yuharu up off the dusty floor of the sanctuary. The sound of his heart in his ears drowned out the sounds of Isolde's fading protests—it was like a drumbeat, faster and faster and faster, battering at his ribs so hard, he thought his whole body might give out. He pushed past the dazed Ōya-Keeper, ran straight into the straggling crowds of tourists and ticket-takers and mascots at the heart of the New Ryūgū-jō. He spotted Mukashi on the other side of the faded red gate—very faraway.

Too far.

But it didn't matter. Kohei ran. His feet pounded the ground, but he didn't feel the pain he knew was shooting up through his ankle bones; he knew he was gasping for breath, but he didn't feel a single bead of sweat on his forehead or in his eyes, didn't notice that his vision was blurred with salt.

He. Just. Ran.

Mukashi ran too—if he went too slowly, someone might notice that he wasn't a kid in a mascot costume. When he picked up enough speed, he didn't look like a ryū at all; he became a flicker of dark scales and a glint of fur. He was surprisingly fast; it was as if his age had only made him stronger. Kohei knew he wouldn't be able to keep up with him for long, but still his legs kept pumping. He wasn't sure if he'd ever be able to stop; he'd probably either crash into a wall or shoot straight off a pier and into the ocean.

He hurtled past all the market vendors, all the ambling tourists. He shoved his way through stacks of

boxes and crates, not bothering to look back or apologize for startling passersby. He didn't care that it was broad daylight, or that the townspeople were likely wondering what had gotten into him—all he cared about was getting Papa back. He could see Mukashi's long, lean body in the distance, his plumes of golden hair, his dark scales. He had small wings, like most ryū, but he still looked strange and primordial, even from the back.

The docks came into view. Kohei smelled the ocean. Salt.

It was like being shoved off of his tightrope, the sudden drop making his stomach lurch up into his throat. Of course—of course, Mukashi lived underwater. In all the oldest mukashi banashi—folk stories—Ryūgū-jō was in the darkest depths of the ocean, ruled over by a fearsome god. It was a place that even time could barely touch.

And Kohei was not time. He was a ten-year-old boy, and he was so exhausted, it took every ounce of strength he had to keep his knees from buckling as he stumbled to the edge of the pier.

The dark sea-foam rippled gently in Mukashi's wake.

After a few moments—Kohei didn't know how long exactly—there were footsteps on the worn, wooden planks behind him—fast, anxious ones. Isolde. Kohei turned to her as she slowed, huffing and red-faced, to see that she had all three of their dragons with her. Including

Yuharu. Kohei was sure that his ryū was indignant and hurt over being left behind, but at the moment, he couldn't bring himself to look at her.

He didn't want to look at anything. Not anymore.

"Kohei," Isolde was saying. *"Kohei!"*

"He's got that look," said Yuharu. "Last time he looked like that, he got in a fistfight with his kindergarten teacher. And won."

Kohei tried to close his hands into fists, but his fingers were clammy, too cold and numb to listen to his brain.

"Kohei?" Isolde said tentatively. "Um . . . are you . . . okay?"

No.

"NO!" Kohei whirled around to glare at her, and there was a part of him that hoped that his fury would warm him. He wanted his hands to thaw into fists; he wanted the bone-deep numbness to go away. Burning would be so much better.

It didn't work.

"Daijōbu janai! Janai! Nothing—*nothing* is ever, ever, *ever* okay!"

"Kohei," said one of their voices.

"Just *stop*." Kohei's head dropped, and his shoulders

hunched like shrapnel was falling from the sky. "Things are broken. Everything is wrong."

He turned back to face the ocean. It was still there, vast and deep and so very much like the end of the world.

No human could ever conquer the ocean. Water could wait out anything, and it made its own way.

Except.

Kohei felt around in his pocket—not the empty one where Papa's lighter was supposed to be, but the other one. The one he'd nearly forgotten about through all this. His fingers closed around his stolen bundle of dried rohai stalks, and all of a sudden, he could feel the bones of his hand beginning to thaw.

It was hope, maybe.

He could see more clearly now. He could see the lines of worry on Isolde's face, the confusion on Naomi's. And Yuharu—well, Yuharu just looked concerned. "Kohei," she said, with the tone of someone trying to negotiate with a heavily armed toddler. "What are you doing? Tell us what you're doing."

"Rohai," Kohei murmured.

"What—the *poison?*" said Isolde.

"It's not just poison," Yuharu told her. It wasn't possible for a ryū to look pale with worry, but she almost seemed to pull it off. "It can help people breathe underwater. But—"

"Kohei, that's absurd!" Isolde exclaimed.

"No, it's not." Kohei's brow furrowed. "*This* leaf . . ." He tapped the smaller one with his thumb. "This one has a very strong dose—it would hurt me. But *this* one . . ."

It was difficult to describe what he was sensing—or how, or *why*. Which, of course, meant that Isolde, Cheshire, and Yuharu thought he was on the verge of a mental breakdown. But he wasn't. His mind was perfectly clear.

What was it about the small leaf that *felt* more poisonous than the big one?

Kohei rubbed the less poisonous leaf between his thumb and pointer finger. "I can't explain it," he said.

"There's nothing to explain," said Yuharu. "Just put the leaves down."

He waved her off. "I think it's the smell," he said. He wasn't sure why he said it, but as soon as the words were out of his mouth, he knew that they were right. "Yes, it's the smell! I know this smell!"

Isolde and Cheshire exchanged a glance.

"No, really." Kohei's brow furrowed in concentration. "I can't name it, but it's—it's like when you hear a lullaby you haven't heard since you were a baby." He detached the big leaf from the stalk, tossing the rest of the plant—which *was* poison, he was sure of it—into the ocean below. He raised the leaf to his nose. "It smells like *Papa*."

Yuharu stiffened. "What do you mean?" she asked.

Kohei pressed the leaf against his forehead, squeezing his eyes shut. In his mind, clear as day, he felt the rough tweed of Papa's blazer against his face. And he heard Papa's voice, clearer than all his other memories—well, all but one.

Gaman, gaman, his father whispered. *Endure with dignity, always. You are more than the world will ever know.*

The smell of rohai leaf was like clean laundry and blankets and fog, and the wistfulness that comes with knowing you've lost something you can't quite remember. It was mittens on a cold day, the crunch of snow, the sound of ice sheets falling . . .

That was Papa's smell.

"What does your father have to do with poison?" Isolde asked, her voice piercing the fabric of Kohei's memory.

Kohei shook his head, not wanting to open his eyes. "Not poison," he said. "That's how I know—the smaller leaf smelled like poison. It was too strong—warm and bitter and sweet. But this one . . ."

Gaman. Yamenaide. Gaman.

Why would Papa have taught Kohei to recognize the smell of rohai leaf?

Maybe, said a small voice in Kohei's head, *he was preparing you.*

Maybe he knew you'd have to swim to Ryūgū-jō someday.

Maybe he saw the kind of life you'd lead, and he wanted to help you, to stay with you. Even though—

Even though Papa drowned.

Papa *drowned*.

Kohei had never been sure until now; his memories from that time were unstable, half-faded. But that night at the hospital . . . Mama answering the phone. Stepping into the intensive care ward. Seeing Papa. A hand squeezing Kohei's. And those papers Ojiisan signed—battered, stapled documents that legally changed Kohei's name from Arahata to Fujiwara . . .

And the smell of rohai leaf. Lingering grief over something not quite forgotten.

Papa researched rohai, and Papa dove into the ocean, and Papa drowned.

Yuharu and Isolde were still talking—even Cheshire added a few words now and then—but it didn't matter. Kohei hardly heard them. He knew with absolute surety that, somehow, *this* was where his life was meant to lead.

Yamenaide—*do not quit.*

Shikata ga *aru—there* are *things you can do.*

Gaman, gaman, gaman—*you are more than the world will ever know.*

Kohei pressed the rohai leaf under his tongue, and dove.

11
The Lonesome God

There was a moment when his throat felt like it was twisting tighter, then expanding. Then he felt a strange pressure in his whole body, like he might burst into a million shattering pieces.

Then some boundary snapped—and Kohei was free.

That's what it was like to breathe underwater. Freedom. Like a weight had been lifted from Kohei's chest, and for the first time in his life, he could actually move. Like *really* move. Water went into his mouth and nose, but it wasn't heavy, and it didn't feel wet. He didn't choke and his eyes didn't burn.

It was magnificent. Vaguely, Kohei wondered why anyone would think that something like this could be a poison.

Yuharu's talons were digging into his shoulder—she must've jumped into the water after him. Of course she had! She'd always been at his side. He kept one hand on her body as he swam, just to make sure she didn't lose her grip and float away, but he knew, somehow, that he didn't have to worry for her. He could feel the magical energy racing through her body. This was her ancestral home, after all—all Eastern ryū were descended from the ocean gods. Even the smallest fragments, ryū on the farthest branches of the family tree, could feel the wholeness of the surging sea. And Yuharu was not a small fragment. She was a very small, very *big* piece of the world.

Kohei blinked. His mind was loopy. Maybe that was what "poison" did—it made you forget your troubles, forget the pain, forget all the things you still had to do. But he couldn't afford to forget. Not now.

He needed to remember the weight of the ocean. The bone-deep thrumming of lost things.

So. Where was he? How long had he been sinking?

A while, apparently. Kohei's feet brushed the ocean floor as he looked around. His surroundings weren't vibrant, but they weren't quite *dull* either; this was a vast, shadowy blue-gray world. It shared its desolate beauty with its children, those quiet-and-loud ōyatama. There was no sunlight this far down, no light apart from Yuharu's ocean-magic glow. Beyond that was an endless mass of water

that looked solid as glass, yet rushed in bubbles, pulsed like a heart.

Yuharu tightened her talons to get Kohei's attention. "There," she whispered. It was a weird, underwater whisper that sounded mostly like bubbles. Everything was muffled down here, less sharp, but somehow more important.

Mukashi. Kohei squinted, trying to focus—thankfully, the old ryū wasn't running anymore. He was resting quietly under a large, rocky overhang near the ocean floor. He probably thought he wasn't being chased. He thought Kohei was a liar, but even liars weren't foolish enough to swallow potentially poisonous leaves and dive into the deepest depths of the ocean just to get a lighter back from an ancient beast.

Well, joke's on him, Kohei thought. *I did it anyway.*

Kohei's vision was blurrier than usual, so once Mukashi started swimming again, Yuharu had to guide them in the right direction by yanking Kohei's ear when he paddled the wrong way. Kohei could feel her impatience—she could've caught Mukashi on her own, easy-peasy-lemon-whatever.

But they couldn't risk being separated. Mukashi went farther and farther, and the ocean floor sloped deeper, delving down into the dark. Even with the power of the rohai leaf coursing through his system, Kohei wondered what would happen if the effects wore off too soon.

Ryūgū-jō—the *real* one—was at the very, very bottom of the ocean. Did that mean that there wouldn't be any oxygen once he got inside? Mukashi was able to breathe air on land, but that didn't mean he *needed* to. He could survive underwater, like Yuharu. Cheshire and Isolde and Kohei—and possibly Naomi—were another story.

What would it be like to suddenly need oxygen in the depths of a churning, endless ocean?

The thought of choking on saltwater a million miles from home was pretty distracting, but all those worries dissolved when the silhouette of Old Ryūgū-jō came into view.

The painting of Ryūgū-jō in Kohei's old picture book was beautiful and elegant and smooth. And flat. It had never felt real to him, no matter how badly he wanted it to be. He could never make it *real*.

But this palace—this real, glowing monument of red and white and gold—was not flat, and it was not smooth. No—when Kohei squinted to see its highest peaks and spirals, wavering like the sparkles of a distant sun, all he could think was that it was rough—*so* rough. Sharp edges and gnarled branches. Brutal yet beautiful. It was ancient, and it was *wonderful*.

Mukashi slowed down when they got close enough to see the palace's illuminated colors. His tail swooshed, and he nodded greetings to other ryū—yes, *other ryū*—as he passed them. Kohei goggled at them as well. They weren't as big as the ones in his impossible memory—actually, most of them were a little smaller than Mukashi—but they were still much bigger than Yuharu. And their scales were so many vibrant shades: red and blue and blue-green, with golden eyes that radiated the strength of the ocean's tides.

Ōki-na ryū. *Big ryū.* The biggest Kohei had ever seen, at least.

They were alive. And they were *here.*

Kohei knew he had no chance of staying hidden as they drew closer to the gates of Ryūgū-jō, so he paddled frantically to close the distance between himself and Mukashi (who, by the way, no longer looked so very grand *or* so very old). The cavernous doors of the palace made the big ryū look like a child. Kohei could only imagine what he and Yuharu looked like. Probably ants. Or fleas.

Or maybe nothing at all.

As they passed through the gates, Kohei stumbled onto impossibly dry land—the water somehow ended at the palace's front staircase. He crashed onto the stone steps, suddenly sopping wet and gasping, surrounded on all sides by oxygen he couldn't remember how to use.

A large paw dragged him to his feet.

Mukashi.

The old ryū peered at him. "Did you follow me all this way?" he demanded.

Kohei was trembling like a leaf, wheezing—*how were lungs supposed to work again?*—but he drew himself up to his full height and tipped his chin up in defiance. "*Yes,*" he gasped, swiping seawater from his forehead. "I *did.*"

He expected Mukashi to roll his eyes, or hit him over the head, or at least make a cryptic-yet-condescending remark about human intelligence. But the old ryū did none of those things. Actually, *he* was the one who looked like he'd taken a blow to the head. He kept staring at Kohei, but the anger had gone out of him, replaced with astonishment and something else, something that made Kohei's heart hurt.

"It's you," Mukashi said hoarsely. "Arahata. You're *Arahata.*"

Last time someone called Kohei by his father's name, it had been an insult, and one that Kohei hadn't fully understood. But Mukashi said it differently. He said *Arahata* like it meant something important, something sacred, something beautiful but also a little bit sad. And the way his eyes softened with recognition made Kohei think of himself, just for a moment, as something important and sacred and beautiful and sad too. Not brutal—not like he sometimes wanted to be. Not *Arahata* the way his former friends Hisao and Tadashi had said it.

Arahata Kohei.

"I am," he said.

Mukashi's ancient eyes lingered on him a few seconds longer. Then, finally, he looked away. "You used rohai to come here," he said. "Risky move. You'll need some more, if you're to make it back to the surface alive."

"But—"

"I keep some here in your father's honor—I shall fetch some for you."

"My father's honor . . . ?"

Mukashi pushed through the doors of Ryūgū-jō Palace before Kohei could say another word. Yuharu tightened her hold on his shoulder, a warning and a comfort. "Well," she murmured. "He *did* recognize Denjirō's lighter, didn't he?"

The inside of the palace was filled with oxygen so clear and pure that it made Kohei's head whirl. He breathed deeply, trying to get a sense of his surroundings. Mukashi had led him into a room, a *big* room, lined with pillars of ivory and jade, gilded with a thousand metallic shades, draped with heavy crimson silk. When Kohei looked up, he had to blink a few times to figure out if he could actually see the ceiling—it was all clouds and shadows up there, a dizzying swirl of coral and stardust. His head was still spinning too much to focus for long. He looked away and squeezed his eyes shut, trying to remember which way was down.

When he opened his eyes with a slightly clearer head, he realized that the clouds and shadows and coral and stardust were not the ceiling.

They were a *ryū*.

No, not a ryū—

A *god*.

The swirl of underwater shadows and stardust looked like a giant ryū, until it didn't. Its wings were as vast as the sky, but then they shifted like smoke. Its coiled body was as thick as the thickest tree trunk, but when Kohei blinked, he realized that *it* didn't move—the air inside the palace shifted out of its way in sheets, undulating like water, showing the *shape* of the god. The god itself had no shape. It had no body. Only the lack of a body.

Was Kohei supposed to bow to it?

He was definitely supposed to bow, right?

How could he bow to something that was directly *above* him?

Mukashi re-emerged from behind one of the silk draperies, carrying a small, square cushion. "Stay here while I fetch your rohai leaves," he ordered Kohei. He placed the pillow on the marble floor and forced Kohei to sit.

"But—I—that—" Kohei glanced up at the ryū-like god above him. He felt utterly out of sorts.

Mukashi followed his gaze. "Ah," he said. He touched Kohei's shoulder, very gently. "That is Ryuuji-sama," he said, using the highest honorific form of address. "Ryūjin, Ōwatatsumikami, possessor of the sea, son of Izanagi and Izanami, brother to the sun god Amaterasu. Ryūgū-jō is his domain . . . but don't worry. He's actually quite friendly."

Mukashi patted Kohei's head, turned, and left.

The room was uncannily quiet.

Kohei felt like a little kid who'd gotten sent to the headmaster office. Like that time he'd punched his kindergarten teacher in the stomach, and the school called his mother for an emergency conference, but Mama was halfway across town, so it took her *forever* to arrive, so Kohei had to *sit* there in front of a whole bunch of angry-looking grown-ups, wondering what they'd do to punish him. In this case, the headmaster was an ancient deity, and his school was the Pacific Ocean, but the feeling of dread was the same—Kohei was sure he'd done something very, very wrong.

He took Yuharu into his hands and held her close to his chest, wanting to keep her near his heart. She was trembling too, and her scales glowed like the moon, glimmering the way they had before, only *brighter* now. *So much brighter.*

They waited together.

Ryuuji-sama said nothing.

Kohei was relieved when one of the palace servants swam by. It was a ryūgū no tsukai—an oarfish—but it didn't seem particularly bothered by the fact that it was moving through air instead of water. It wasn't there for Kohei—it zoomed through a side door and didn't return. Then another pair of oarfish came by, and left again, with a Mukashi-sized ryū and its young apprentice ryū scurrying in its wake. Kohei watched them all, puzzled—apparently something interesting was happening. Did it have anything to do with him?

He hoped not. Oarfish weren't very expressive—few fish were—but he thought the ones swimming by looked pretty worried.

Kohei shifted in place, hugging Yuharu tighter. He looked up at Ryuuji, still swirling above his head. "Ōwatatsumikami-sama?" he said, trying to get the god's attention without actually *getting* his attention.

And just like that, Ryuuji drew himself into the physical form of a ryū—an incredibly big ryū, like the ones in Kohei's impossible memory—and lowered his head to the floor, coiling his body upward so that it filled most of the room. Kohei bowed his own head. "I am sorry to be a nuisance to you," he whispered. "May I intrude, and ask a question of you?"

Ryuuji nodded, his whiskers undulating like ocean waves.

"I—I—humbly—" Kohei couldn't think straight, not with a literal god staring directly at him. All his formalities fell away. "Sir, *what* are all these creatures doing?" he blurted out. "Where are they going? And *why?*"

Ryuuji raised one eyebrow. "You think they'd ever tell me?" he rumbled in his earthquake voice, tipping his head at one of the worried-looking oarfish as it wriggled frantically past.

"They don't work for you?" Kohei asked.

"Oh, they do. But I am a god." Ryuuji sighed, and the space around him sighed too, shifting out in waves. "They respect me, worship me . . . and set me apart. When I was younger, an eternity ago, being distant made me proud. But now I am not so sure. It seems I matter so much to them that *I* matter nothing at all."

"Oh," said Kohei. "That's sad."

"And what is your name, child?"

Fujiwara came to Kohei's lips first, out of habit. But in this palace of coral and shadows, he did not feel like a Fujiwara, not anymore. "Arahata Kohei to mōshimasu," he said. The words reminded him of the first time he'd introduced himself to Isolde, and he almost smiled. "Yoroshiku onegai itashimasu."

"Arahata-san," Ryuuji said. "Look at me."

"Sir?"

"Look me in the eye."

Kohei looked up. Ryuuji's physical features were typical for a ryū—gilded blue scales, silky whiskers. But his eyes were entirely godlike, still that swirl of dark and fog and shadow and starlight. Each was the size of Kohei's head. They made him feel small but also very precious somehow—like even if he was a raindrop compared to this vast ocean spirit, he still mattered a great deal, because he was a raindrop named *Kohei*.

"Tell me a story, Arahata-kun," Ryuuji said.

"A story?" said Kohei.

"A good one."

"Ryuuji-sama, you must know more stories than I do!"

Ryuuji laughed. "Oh, certainly I do!" he said. "I know more stories than anyone below the heavens. But those are not *your* stories, are they? And I am so tired of hearing things I know. Tell me a story, please," he repeated, more urgently this time. "Tell me one I have not heard before. It's been so long since we've had a visitor, let alone a human."

Kohei was speechless. What could *he* offer an immortal deity?

What did he know that the god of the sea did not?

"Well—when I was little," Kohei began before he could stop himself, "there was this stray cat that would hunt on our street, and I called him Mr. Mousie . . ."

The words came tumbling out. For the first time, Kohei realized how much stories hated staying untold. And Ryuuji-sama seemed entertained—he even laughed now and then—so Kohei kept talking:

The time Mama baked a cake with salt instead of sugar . . .

The time Kohei snuck outside in the middle of the night to play alone in the snow . . .

The time Mr. Mousie stole Yuharu's pouch of sakura petals, and she challenged him to a duel . . .

The time Kohei fell down the stairs, and Ojiisan picked him up and hugged him close and wanted to keep him safe.

All the worried oarfish and hurrying ryū servants faded away, and the world was only Ryuuji, and Kohei and his stories, and Yuharu's small interjections, which became bolder and bolder as she grew more accustomed to speaking in front of her ancient ancestor.

When Kohei finally trailed off, Ryuuji let out a wistful sigh. "You have such important memories," he said.

He sounded jealous. Like Kohei had something precious, something constantly out of reach. Maybe memories were less special to someone who had so many—it must be awful, to be a god.

Suddenly, all Kohei wanted was to offer Ryuuji-sama

one more precious thing. "Don't worry!" he exclaimed. "I have another memory. It's an old one—a special one!"

An impossible one.

"Wrong."

Kohei halted halfway through his sentence—*wrong?* He'd only just gotten to the part where he looked up and saw the Western dragon circling in the sky. Ryuuji hadn't interrupted any of the other stories, not even the embellished ones about Yuharu fighting gangs of stray cats. And now he was saying—

"You have it *wrong.*" Ryuuji's stardust eyes, which had danced with laughter just moments before, now looked like vast orbs of ash.

Kohei had no idea what to say. He fell back on honorific speech to give his brain some time to come up with actual thoughts. "Sir, perhaps I have been incorrect, however—"

Ryuuji's thick, coiling body began to rise, slowly, up, up, up toward the grand ceiling of Ryūgū-jō. *The god wasn't angry*, Kohei thought—the palace wasn't quaking or rumbling, and Ryuuji's eyes didn't turn red or fiery or anything. They stayed blank. Like dust.

Which was so, so much worse.

Yuharu shifted, taking shelter at the nape of Kohei's neck. "Kohei . . . ?" she whispered.

Ryuuji shifted, spread, and dissolved once more into the high-up shadows. "That is not your memory," his voice boomed. The words came from all around, like they were built into the very walls of the palace. "It is a half-told story, and it is *wrong*."

"I don't understand," Kohei said.

"Do you want to see?"

Before Kohei could draw breath to answer, Ryuuji— the shadows, the stardust, the palace walls—collapsed in on him, and everything whooshed and whirled like smoke, and then, suddenly, Kohei was there, in the midst of a jostling crowd.

In his impossible memory.

It was just as it had always been: a bright, clear day in that part of winter that isn't quite winter anymore—coldness with a hint of warmth, warmth you can't *feel*, but which seems to change the air anyway. And there was Ojiisan. His hair was darker, and his eyes were clearer, and the big ryū were here.

Except . . .

Except if the big ryū were here, it was the end of the

war. And the war hadn't ended in late winter or almost-spring. Hiroshima and Nagasaki were destroyed by atom-drakes in late August . . . so this memory should've been in—

September.

Ryuuji's claw touched Kohei's shoulder. "Try again," he said.

It was just as it had always been, but now he saw that they were in early autumn, not late winter, and there were no changing leaves on the trees. There were no leaves at all. The branches were stripped bare, groping at the sky like they couldn't feel their own roots in the soil.

It was quieter too. Without the crunch of dried leaves on the ground, all Kohei heard was the crunch of the big ryū's talons against the cracked asphalt. Except—

Kohei realized for the first time that he'd never actually looked at the road. He'd only ever gazed up at the ryū, and sometimes studied Ojiisan's face. What would happen if he looked down?

"Look down, Kohei," Ryuuji said.

Kohei didn't want to.

"Look *down.*"

He looked.

The asphalt was not cracked, because the roads were not paved. They'd been stripped down to bare, burnt soil. It was the big ryū's talons that crunched. The *talons*. They were broken, split to the root. They twisted with every lumbering step, scraping painfully against the bomb-beaten earth.

"Look up," said Ryuuji.

Kohei looked up, the world spinning around him in sudden movement, and with a sense of relief, he saw the Western dragon in the sky above, circling like a hawk, protecting everyone on the ground below like he'd always remembered.

Except.

Except circling hawks did not protect. And neither did Americans.

"Try again," said Ryuuji.

Here Kohei was. The lumbering big ryū, unearthly and emotionless, trudged through the crowd of betrayed, soot-smudged onlookers. The ryū's fur was matted, their eyes dark voids. And in the sky above, the Western dragon—the *executioner*—circled, surveying its masterwork.

It was a dim, quiet sort of nightmare.

Kohei found his grandfather in the crowd. Ojiisan's face looked the same as it always had as he gazed up at the broken, majestic ryū for the last time, his eyes filled with an unrecognizable emotion. But for the first time, Kohei realized that he *did* recognize it, and always had.

Not love. *Resignation.* It was the same look Mama got while sweeping glass shards under the rug in the morning, when she looked up and saw Kohei and promised him his breakfast.

Not love.

Shikata ga nai. There's nothing that can be done.

And here Kohei was, in real life again, facing Ryuuji—who was not shadows or dust anymore, just a very large ryū— in the grand emptiness of the Old Ryūgū-jō. Here Kohei was, with the reality of his impossible memory staring him in the face. Because he couldn't have remembered—and so he hadn't. He hadn't wanted to.

But now he needed to.

Ryuuji opened his massive mouth like he wanted to say more. But Kohei would not let him. Instead, he lunged forward, craning his neck to look the ryū-god in both eyes. "Why?" he demanded.

Ryuuji did not respond.

Kohei swallowed and was surprised by how much it hurt. It was hard to talk, but harder to cry. "I don't understand," he choked out. *"Why?"*

Ryuuji's whole body wavered like the ocean. He stared at Kohei with empty eyes.

Kohei shook his head and turned away, wiping the half-formed tears from his eyes. He'd wasted too much time here with Ryuuji—he should've been looking for Mukashi, demanding real answers from *him*. Mukashi was the one who'd known his parents. *He* was the one who stole Papa's lighter, who spoke in more riddles than Yuharu ever had.

Kohei intercepted the next servant who came zooming through the grand room, a stout, wide-eyed oarfish messenger. It seemed extremely annoyed to be intercepted by a scrawny little human like Kohei, but it bobbed its head at him anyway. *What do* you *want?* its expression said.

"Answers," Kohei demanded.

An exasperated wriggle: *Oh sure, miniature human. Of course.*

Kohei winced, and not just because Yuharu had nipped his ear in reproach. His words were sharper than they should've been. None of this was the oarfish's fault—it probably had important work to do, and it didn't deserve to be snapped at.

"Sorry," Kohei said. "That was dramatic. I just mean . . ."

He looked around, blinking through his tiredness. "What's going on? Is the palace usually so busy?"

The oarfish snorted, insofar as an oarfish *could* snort, and bobbed its head from side to side. *No.*

"Okay, right, sorry." Kohei bowed his head. "Thank you. I won't keep you any longer."

The oarfish swam away. Kohei was tempted to call it back, to ask—just out of curiosity—if oarfish could speak like the ryū could. But it was none of his business, really. So he stepped back and waited for a Mukashi-sized ryū to come along.

When one did, it was even less enthusiastic about answering Kohei's questions than the oarfish, though it did peer closely at Kohei, as if wondering whether such a small human was worth being curious about.

"What is happening here?" Kohei asked, bowing his head respectfully.

The ryū glanced around. "Do you not know?" he replied. His voice was high-pitched, more wavery than Mukashi's or even Yuharu's, but it still held a note of command. This was *his* home, after all. "I thought *she* was a friend of yours."

"She?" said Kohei. On his shoulder, Yuharu stiffened and curled her claws.

"The little human girl," the ryū said. He shook his head. "Such a pity."

"*Pity? Why* pity?" Kohei felt a rising wave of panic. The *little human girl* could only be Isolde—what had happened to her? Had she come after him? Had she taken too much rohai, or too little, or the wrong kind? He hadn't explained the scents of the leaves well enough—he hadn't expected her to dive into the ocean for him, after all.

Of course, despite the bone-numbing alarm at the thought of Isolde getting hurt, some small, guilty part of him felt warm too. Because she *had* come for him.

"One of her dragons is extremely ill—took an improper rohai dose," the ryū told him. "All of our healers needed to be called, even those from other oceans. That's why there are so many messengers flying about."

"Oh." Kohei felt like he'd been pushed very hard from a very high-up place. *Was it Cheshire?* The thought made him want to crawl into an underwater cave and never come out. *Isolde's* Cheshire? The dragon she took care of, and who took care of her?

Who knew a language that so few living people knew . . .

Kohei coughed. "Which?" he croaked. "The Western dragon?"

The wavery-voiced ryū gave him a withering look. "We could've dealt with a Western dragon's injuries ourselves," he said. "Their biology is entirely conventional. No, it's the other one—the East-and-West one. We've never treated a creature like her before and are unsure of how to proceed."

"Oh," Kohei said. "But Naomi's no different from you, not really—she's like any other ryū."

As soon as he'd said those words, Kohei wanted to crawl into a cave. *Like any other ryū?* How could he *say* that? Naomi wasn't like any other *anything*—she was Naomi, with her big, intelligent eyes and her waggly tail. Naomi, who loved making people laugh, even though she was just a baby.

The big ryū standing before him knew what he'd meant, though, and his annoyed gaze softened. "I know," the ryū said. "And we're doing our best for her, I promise. But I have to go now—I have work to do."

The ryū dashed away, his long, tufted tail flapping in his wake.

Kohei reached up to touch Yuharu's head, just to make sure that she was there. She was, of course—she always was.

So why did Kohei feel so alone?

He turned back to look at Ryuuji—to ask for help, or maybe just to hear that deep, reassuring voice.

But Ryuuji had turned to mist and had risen back to the ceiling. He could not be a part of this story.

He was only a god.

12
Histories

*A*s Kohei *wandered* through the sprawling hallways of an ancient, undersea ryū palace, all he could think about was drowning.

Choking.

Flailing, floundering, and then . . . nothing.

Like Papa.

He tried to focus on all the wonderfully fancy decor—the glint of gold-leaf calligraphy on the walls, the wavering flame of lantern light . . .

Naomi was just a baby.

The soft, heavy thumping of his sneakers on the crimson carpet . . .

She didn't even know how to talk yet.

The chill of the air against his tear-stained cheeks, how the stillness and the quiet made him feel like he was in a museum . . .

She couldn't cry for help.

The stretched-out corridors that seemed to go on forever, twisting and turning, going deeper and deeper into the bedrock of the planet . . .

She must've been so scared.

Just like Papa.

Papa, who'd wanted to come back home, who'd been swimming, struggling, reaching for Kohei, wanting to find him. Wanting to save him.

Wanting to *help* him.

Like Isolde and Naomi had.

Kohei wheeled around midstep and kicked the nearest vase as hard as he could. It was an old, grand thing, nearly as tall as he was, made of heavy, white porcelain like the artifacts Kohei had seen in pictures of China. Yuharu yelped, lunging from his shoulder to stop it from falling, but she was too small to reach it in time. It hit the ground with an echoing *CRACK*, splitting in two against the crimson floor.

"Kohei!" Yuharu exclaimed. "Why would you—"

Kohei ignored her. He kicked the porcelain fragments, then turned and kicked the opposite wall, even

though his toe was already throbbing, and when all of *that* didn't make him feel better, he punched the wall as hard as he could and tore down a glimmering silk tapestry, wringing it like a dish towel.

Yuharu was shouting something urgent in his ear, but Kohei couldn't hear her through the pounding in his skull. He didn't *want* to hear her. He tried to shred the fabric of the tapestry, but it was fine silk, and he couldn't, so he flung it to the floor and stamped on it, over and over and over again until his foot felt like it was on fire.

And then he spun around and collided with Mukashi.

It was like striding face-first into the side of a mountain. Kohei jerked back, reeling, and Mukashi reached to steady him with one large paw. "There you are," the big ryū said. His voice was casual, like he hadn't just found Kohei committing felony-level vandalism. "I was looking for you. Your friend—the little girl—"

"*Isolde*," Kohei interrupted.

Mukashi's grip tightened. ". . . is waiting in the gardens to the north of the palace," he finished. "Would you like me to show you the way?"

"That would be lovely," said Yuharu.

"Absolutely *not*," Kohei snarled.

Yuharu sighed.

Mukashi gave them both an odd look. "Ryūgū-jō is a complicated place," he said, a note of warning in his words.

"Even the wisest of ryū sometimes have trouble navigating it without help."

"I don't want your help. I want the *truth*." Kohei drew himself to his full height and glared for all he was worth, just like Isolde would have. Mukashi was old and wise, but Kohei was young and fierce, and he knew from speaking to Ryuuji that he did not need to be afraid.

"The truth," said Mukashi.

"Yes."

"I have not lied to you."

"But you haven't told me everything yet either," Kohei said. "That counts."

"Mmm." Mukashi looked skeptical. "You might not *want* to hear everything. Did that ever occur to you?"

"I'm an Arahata, like you said. I'll never stop wanting to know."

A shadow crossed Mukashi's face. "No," he said. "I suppose you won't."

"He *really* won't," Yuharu muttered.

Mukashi tipped his head from side to side, considering his options. Then, he motioned for Kohei to follow him. "Walk with me," he said. "We'll take the long way to the northern gardens."

"So," Mukashi said as he led Kohei and Yuharu down a set of wider, newer-looking hallways. "Kohei, or Sōseki?"

"Eh?" Kohei said, startled.

"Your name."

"Oh . . . Kohei."

Mukashi nodded thoughtfully. "Your father always said he wanted two sons," he said. "One named Kohei, after his grandfather, and the other named Sōseki, after the famous novelist."

"You knew Kohei's father well," Yuharu said.

"Mmm." Mukashi hardly seemed to hear her—his gaze was fixed somewhere in the middle distance as he led them around a corner. "Of course," he muttered to himself, "Kyōsuke would have insisted on an ancestral name . . ."

"Did you know my grandfather too?" Kohei asked.

"Eh? Kyo? Oh, of course!" Mukashi shook himself out of his reverie. "I have known Kyo since the day he was born. March 11, 1900 . . . I swore to protect him, always." Mukashi glanced at Kohei and Yuharu. "I was barely a year old myself, but ryū have long lives and even longer memories."

"Oh," said Kohei. His head felt a bit like a balloon, bobbing farther and farther away from the rest of his body. "You—*you* were my grandfather's ryū? His own, I mean—*his?* You're not *dead?* I thought . . ."

Mukashi didn't say a word.

"You knew him." Kohei shook his head, trying to

shake away the floaty balloon feeling. "What was he like when he was younger? Was he like me? Was he like *Mama?* And what was *Mama* like? Was she always so quiet, or was she like me too? What did she—"

Mukashi held up one paw, stemming the flood of questions.

"Your grandfather's godfather was Chihaya Kōhei," he said after a pause. "Chihaya was your namesake, and your father's grandfather. The Arahata and Fujiwara families were close friends to one another for decades, you see, long before your parents wed." He glanced at Kohei. "That was why, when your father earned a spot at a medical school near Ōsaka, Kyōsuke offered him a place to stay, in his spare room."

"Which is where he met Mama," Kohei said. He'd heard this part of the story before.

Mukashi reached into the pouch around his neck—it was like the one Yuharu carried, but much bigger, and with fewer flower petals—and withdrew Papa's lighter. Kohei's heart leapt at the sight of it.

"Here," Mukashi said, handing it back reluctantly. "This belonged to Chihaya Kōhei, but your father was responsible for the inscription. Do you know what those two characters mean?"

Kohei tilted the silver weight in his hand, watching the light dance across the engraved surface. "Of course,"

he said. "Papa wrote it in his notes too. In the margins of Dr. Arima's books."

"Ah." Mukashi halted. "So, that's where you learned the fire trick."

"Did you know Dr. Arima too? I think he was Papa's friend."

Mukashi thought for a long time, looking at the walls, the hallway floor . . . anywhere but Kohei's face.

"Did you know that your father didn't fight in the war?" he asked, finally.

"Yes," Kohei said. He was puzzled by the sudden change in subject. "He was an only son and a medical student—Mama said that made him doubly exempt."

"Yes. And Dr. Arima was a medical student too, an older classmate of your father's. He was recruited to work for the military, designing weapons . . . and weaponizing ryū." Mukashi's expression darkened. "He engineered our hatchlings to be bigger by heating the ōyatama before they hatched. The government wanted their battle-ryū to be as big as Ryuuji—as big as the ryū-gods of myth. The Imperial government was so in love with those old legends of chaos and war. Arima was the same."

"That doesn't sound like Papa," Kohei said.

"Oh, no. Your father was furious with Dr. Arima. He said that scientists were meant to heal people, not hurt them. That was why the Emperor thought Arahata Denjirō was dangerous . . . not because he was angry, or violent, but because he was kind.

"Between his classes, your father started reading about empires outside of Japan, and how they'd fallen. He collected all sorts of history books from France, Italy, Russia. He and your grandfather would debate for hours, late into the night. Your father argued for democracy, and he usually won—he was young, and very educated, you know." Mukashi laughed, a happy, weepy sound. "He had the sharpest tongue of anyone I've ever known!"

Kohei could imagine that, and the thought made him smile too—Papa, focused and passionate, declaring *Liberté, égalité, fraternité!* while Ojiisan shook his head and grumbled. Late into the night, lanterns burning low, lots of half-empty sake cups strewn across the table . . . Papa's collar would've been askew, Ojiisan's dark hair sticking up in all different directions . . .

"Kyōsuke might have tolerated him," Mukashi added, "if not for his daughter."

Mama.

"Your mother was young, and impulsive, and passionate. She loved your father and his ideas. And one day, she told your grandfather that she hoped there was a revolution— that if Denjirō took up arms against the Emperor, she would follow him.

"Saying that kind of thing could've gotten her killed in those days, had the wrong person overheard."

Kohei could imagine that too. He'd heard awful stories of the Kenpeitai—the murderous Imperial police—and the Tokkō, who were in charge of silencing anyone in Japan who disagreed with the war.

He *could* imagine, but he didn't want to.

"So, Kyo panicked." Mukashi's voice held a grim note of finality. "He reported your father to the government, and two days later, Denjirō's office was raided. He was sent into permanent exile."

Kohei could imagine, and despite himself, he did.

Papa's office. Not the one Kohei knew, perhaps, but another, similar office, full of books and dust and things that mattered to Papa. Tokkō officers kicking the door off its hinges, tearing through covers and pages and knocking over shelves, shouting at Papa, grabbing him, beating him. *Hurting* him. Hurting Papa, whose eyes were so kind, whose arms were so strong, whose voice sounded like warm things even when everything was cold . . .

They flung some of the books into a wooden crate—those would be burned. They tossed others aside like they were nothing, like their pages were only paper and ink.

They found the dissertation bound in red cloth.

Rōshia-go, one of them said, rifling through it. *It's in Russian.*

His colleague grabbed it and shoved it in Papa's face. *What is this?* he snarled. *What does it say?*

They didn't let Papa answer before they'd determined his fate.

Kyōsan-tō, they decided. *He's a socialist.*

An agitator.

Dangerous.

"Your mother was displeased, to say the least," Mukashi said. "She and your father were not married yet, but still, she loved him. She'd meant what she said—where Denjirō went, she'd follow."

So they packed their bags and fled in the night. Frantic, but calm. Frightened, but unafraid. Rearranging small objects on their mantelpiece, needing them to be perfect before they left, knowing all the while that they'd never survive the exile that was to come. Clinging to each other against the roaring winds of an invisible hurricane. Tossed around like a crate in the sea as they searched for a safe place to shelter . . .

"Manchuria." Mukashi pronounced it halfway between accents: *manzhuu*. Kohei knew that Northern China was close to Japan; it was certainly closer than New York or Poland. But this was faraway in *time*, not just in space. In his mind, he saw Mama and Papa, trying to make a life. Young and impulsive, but tired now. They smiled for each other. They made friends, sowed seeds, learned bits of other

languages to exchange letters with Dr. Woźnica-Schultz, a colleague of Papa's in Siberia (Kohei's heart squeezed painfully at the sound of yet another lost name).

They prayed for the Imperial government to fall so they could go home. And when it fell?

"Four hundred miles," Mukashi said. His words were foggy, like they too had traveled a long distance to reach Kohei's ears. *Four hundred miles, on foot, the first leg of their trip back to what was left of Japan.* They walked up the length of the Chinese coast, all the way to Port Arthur, month after month after month, searching for a way home. That was farther than Kohei and Isolde had traveled, and they'd taken a train. To *walk* all that way?

That was an unfathomable distance. A war-torn distance. It was the distance between Kohei and Ojiisan, and Kohei and *Mama*, and now he understood why.

"You never answered my question, you know," Mukashi said.

Question?

"The inscription." The ryū tipped his head at the silver lighter still clutched in Kohei's palm. "Those two characters. Do you know what they mean?"

"Kega."

Mukashi shook his head. "Guài wǒ."

"What?"

"You used the wrong dictionary." Mukashi gestured at the words, sad and knowing and resigned. "Those are not Japanese kanji. They are Chinese Hànzì. Most kanji share their meanings with their original versions, but these are an exception.

"In Mandarin, 'guài' means *blame*. 'Wǒ' means *me*. Those characters were a reminder that your father carried with him, always. He so loved carrying words." Mukashi's voice tightened. "He never forgot that if people were hurting and he stayed silent, he would also carry the blame."

Hurt. Blame me. Similar in a way, but also so very different. Kohei rubbed his sleeve against his cheeks, hating the feel of tears. How could he have been wrong and right at the same time?

Mukashi cleared his throat. "I often think of Denjirō's death," he said. "That's why I collect rohai leaves. He was fascinated with those plants—obsessed with their secrets, like he was preparing for something." Mukashi's bushy eyebrows drew into a frown. "Maybe he was. The last time we saw him . . . it had been thirteen years since the weaponized ryū were executed—thirteen years since the rest of us went into hiding. 1958 . . . you were probably a baby, then, weren't you, Kohei-kun? I doubt you'd remember it."

But Yuharu's talons had tightened on Kohei's shoulder, and Kohei knew why. Because no, he *did* remember that

year. In 1958, he had been three years old. Old enough to remember what Papa's voice sounded like, and to learn the countless smells of rohai leaf.

1958.

The last time Mukashi had seen Papa was the day that he died.

"I remember," Kohei said hollowly. "There was a storm."

Mukashi nodded grimly.

Thirteen years had seemed like long enough, to some ryū—they'd wanted to go back to the surface, to live among humans again. Others, like Mukashi, disagreed. To the people of Japan, big ryū were more than beasts—they were symbols of Imperial power, the kind of power that inspired men to go to war.

"We bickered over it," Mukashi said. "And the bickering turned to arguing, and the arguing turned to fighting." His mouth twisted into a wry grimace. "Big ryū have a tendency to fight; that's why the government was so obsessed with breeding us bigger and bigger during the war, and why so many of us complied. We can be powerful weapons.

"As we grew angrier, the waters of the seas heated, and the winds began to pick up. Denjirō must've recognized what that meant."

Because in the thick of the fighting, Papa had showed up at the palace gates.

He'd used rohai, like Kohei. Mukashi hadn't seen him

in so long, he hardly recognized him. But even though Denjirō's hair was gray and his eyes were lined with sorrow, he still tipped his chin up and looked Mukashi straight in the eye like he had when he was young.

Papa got up in front of the big ryū, and he told them they could *not* come back. He explained what things were like, back on land. He spoke of chaos and destruction and grief. And he spoke of his son . . . his quiet, thoughtful, sensitive son.

Yuharu squeezed Kohei's shoulder again, gentler this time.

Mukashi's paw twitched. "Denjirō told us how he'd immersed himself in his work, knowing that it would be needed," he said. "Knowing that, someday, the ryū of Ryūgū-jō would forget—that we would try to come back to the surface, despite it all. He said he knew someone would have to come to reason with us, to stop us. And he did. He was always so persuasive, our Denjirō."

Papa reminded the ryū of the consequences of a nation's pride. And then he left.

And he was swept away by a storm that could've drowned a dozen full-sized ryū, never mind one brave, tired man.

Kohei shuddered. He had a few photographs of Papa, but it was these stories that made him real—stories that Mama scarcely told, because they hurt so much.

"You'll have to hear the rest from your mother," Mukashi said, as though he'd read Kohei's thoughts. "She'll know more than I do. But—" He faltered. "Your grandfather—my Kyo. Tell me, is he all right? Has he found happiness without me?"

Kohei shook his head, wiping his eyes even though they were dry. "No," he said.

And even though he had so many thoughts in his head, he couldn't say any more.

Was this how Ojiisan felt? *Wordless?*

No—no, not quite. Kohei looked down at the lighter clasped tight in his hand. It was a gift from his father, something to hold on to—something that could burn him if he wasn't careful but could also keep him warm.

Blame me, it said.

Maybe it wasn't Kohei's fault that he felt alone sometimes, or that the grown-ups in his life were angry and afraid. Maybe it wasn't his fault they'd passed their anger and fear down to him. But it wasn't *Papa's* fault that he couldn't fix everything either, because *his* parents had passed a lot of anger and fear down to *him*.

Papa kept trying. That was what mattered. And though the fire of trying hurt him sometimes, it still had the power to fix things too.

It wasn't Kohei's fault that he couldn't fix the world,

but it *was* his responsibility to keep trying. Shikata ga *aru*—he would never stop.

Mukashi cleared his throat as they drew closer to a big, smooth onyx doorway. "Isolde is through here, in the statue garden," he said. "Will you go down to her?"

Ryūgū-jō's gardens were as lovely and impossible as the palace itself. Kohei had read about them in his books when he was little: pink blossoms to the east, rustling red maples to the west, cicadas in the south, and snow-covered crags lining the north.

Isolde and Cheshire were waiting in the snow like Mukashi had said. Kohei found them by a line of ojizōsama figurines—short, round-headed, stone Buddha carvings, all lined up and capped with ice. When Kohei was little, he'd thought that Ojiisan was an ojizōsama, because he was also bald and short, and looked like a mushroom from certain angles.

But Ojiisan was not made of stone. And neither was Isolde. Though from a distance, Kohei thought she looked strangely perfect in the midst of the eddying snowflakes, like maybe she belonged in a place like this, high up on some mountain in the cold and stillness and quiet.

He trudged through the heavy snow to where she sat, her knees drawn up and her head bowed, shards of ice resting on her dark lashes. He brushed snow off of one of the statues and sat down beside her. Isolde didn't say anything, didn't even look at him to say she knew he was there.

But he was.

Kohei pulled Yuharu down from his shoulder, sheltering her from the snow. "You know," he said conversationally, "my father was from a place like this. A snowy place, I mean, not an underwater one."

No response.

"I, uh . . . I've only been to that part of Japan—the snow country—once or twice. And it was when Papa was alive, so I don't remember much. But it was pretty. Like this." Kohei looked up, shielding his eyes against the falling flakes. "It felt faraway, even when I was there. Like a little, frozen piece of the world, where nothing that hurt could reach me anymore."

A smaller city, but an older one. So far to the north. It had been cold, so cold, with snow up to Papa's knees and icicles that were taller than Kohei himself. Kohei shivered.

Papa's parents had lived there. Or maybe they'd died there. Maybe that's why Papa brought Kohei to the snow country—for the osōshiki, the funeral. Kohei remembered a big house, his great-uncle's house, built of stone and paper and wood. There were lots of old things lined up on the lacquer cabinets—photos, carvings.

A broken dish.

Kohei hadn't noticed it at first, because it was such a small and ordinary-looking bowl. But when he looked closer, he saw that the dish had been cracked a few times— it was held together now with metallic lacquer, a spider-web of glittering gold.

Kintsugi, Papa's voice said. The deep sound reached Kohei, even at the bottom of the sea. *Fixing a broken thing with gold. It makes it all the more beautiful, you know, because it's one of a kind. Those fractures tell its story. There is a special beauty in things that are broken, then put back together—things that cannot last forever. Fleeting, fragile.* His hand touched the top of Kohei's head. *And beautiful.*

Before he met Ryuuji, lonely god of the ocean, Kohei would've tried to keep that story of Papa for himself. But Isolde looked like she needed a story. So he gave it to her.

". . . and beautiful," he finished.

Isolde smiled unconvincingly at him. "That's a nice story," she said.

"I've never told it before. But I think I want to start telling things again. To remember."

Isolde's fake smile dissolved. "To remember," she said. *"Right."* She looked down at her hands. "Did they tell you about Naomi?"

Kohei braced himself for the worst. "Is she . . . ?" he began.

"She's alive. But she's not okay." Isolde swallowed, and it looked like she wanted to stop there, but she couldn't; the words tumbled out. "She got sick—when I followed you, I rushed—I gave her the wrong amount of rohai, and it—I mean, I did exactly what *you* did, and we came the same distance, and it was the right amount for Cheshire, but Naomi's so little, so I guess it—I dunno." Isolde sniffled furiously. "She has to stay down here in order to survive. She can't come home. She'll never remember *me*, never hear my stories. We'll probably never see each other again."

Kohei wanted to say something like, *Don't worry, you'll feel better about it someday!* But he saw the look on Isolde's face, and he knew better than to lie.

Isolde rubbed at her eyes. "It's *okay*," she muttered. *Daijōbu.* "Naomi, she's at home here. There are so many other ryū to keep her company. She'll live a good life. Right?"

"Of course," Kohei said. "And you'll always remember her, like Mukashi remembers Ojiisan. Even if she never knows you, she'll be special to you, always. You *made* her. She wouldn't exist without you—that's something, isn't it?"

"I guess," Isolde said.

There was a pause.

"Wait, Mukashi remembers your *grandfather?*"

"Oh yeah—you missed that." It was Kohei's turn to glance away, not wanting Isolde to see the snowflakes on *his* lashes. "He was Ojiisan's ryū. He knew my family. And my father. And he told me . . . things."

"Oh," said Isolde. "What things?"

"Sad things."

"Oh."

Kohei swallowed. "And *happy* things too!" he said, louder than he meant to. "He told me happy things. It was mostly sad, but—but I'm happy that I know. And that makes the sad things a little happy too, maybe—does that make sense?"

"Yes," Isolde said softly. "It does."

The happiness echoed, and the drifts of snow whipped through Kohei's hair, stinging his cheeks with ice.

"Can we go *home?*"

13
Nip the Buds

When you've been to the very depths of the ocean, how do you come back to the surface? How do you learn to breathe air again?

How could Kohei ever go back to the way things were before?

He wasn't quite sure what to expect as the train drew closer to home. There was a part of him that had forgotten how to worry about the future, mostly because he was so tired—when was the last time he'd slept? A month ago? A year?

It didn't matter. The only thing Kohei could focus on was the weight of the unhatched dragon egg in his arms— the one he and Isolde had picked up at the New Ryūgū-jō on their way back to the train station. The Ōya-Keeper was annoyed at being disturbed for the second time that day, but he didn't try to stop them. He just waved a weary hand at them, muttering something about part-time pay.

Kohei blinked and shook his head. He needed to stay awake until he got home—Yuharu was a determined ryū, but she wouldn't be able to drag him off the train if he fell asleep.

It wasn't much longer—the next time the train slowed to a halt, Isolde stirred and Yuharu nudged Kohei with her tail. "We're home," she whispered.

Kohei peered through the smudged glass window, blinking. It was later in the evening than he'd realized, almost dusk. There were shadows cast across the platform, so he didn't recognize, at first—

Mama. Mama was waiting for him. And there were both of Isolde's parents, clutching each other's hands . . . and beside them, a stern-looking man in a stationmaster's uniform, and another figure, the man who'd sold Kohei his train tickets early that morning.

Mrs. Carter looked relieved. Mr. Carter kept all traces of emotion from his expression, though there was a softness in the lines around his eyes that made Kohei's heart hurt. They'd thought Isolde wasn't going to come back.

And Mama . . .

Mama's mouth was twisted into a hard, bitter scowl, the kind that made her look almost like a statue—an *exhausted* statue. She looked so much older than Kohei remembered.

And so much angrier.

"What were you *thinking?*" Mama hissed.

Kohei kept his eyes averted—if he looked at her face, he might throw up. Or faint. "Gomenasai," he murmured in apology.

"You lied to me! You skipped your classes!" She grabbed his shoulder, hard. "You *left.*"

That accusation rang louder than all the others.

Kohei's cheeks flushed. "Kowa garasete—" he began. *Hurt . . .*

"Where did you go?" *Fear.*

"—shimatte—" *Regret.*

"Kohei!" *Rage.*

". . . sumimasen deshita!" *So, so sorry.*

"WHERE?"

Mama never yelled. Mama never yelled. Not at Kohei—not at anyone. There was only one person he'd ever heard her shout at, and that man was still in the hospital.

"Ryūgū-jō," said Kohei.

Mama's face went blank. "You went to *Chiba?*" she said in disbelief. *"Why?"*

"We—" He glanced at Isolde, who was getting an equally harsh scolding from her parents. "We also went to the Old Ryūgū-jō. We swam—*I* swam—I wanted to—"

Mama's eyes widened, and she stared at Kohei without any understanding. "Old Ryūgū-jō," she whispered.

"Yes."

There was a long pause.

"Did you bring scuba gear? Oxygen tanks?"

"No," Kohei said without thinking. "I had rohai leaf. I—"

Mama's eyes went wide with horror. Not anger—fear. It was hard to tell the difference at first, but as Kohei forced himself to meet her gaze, he realized—she'd never yelled at him before because he'd never made her scared.

And she was scared now.

Which, oddly enough, made Kohei's whole body burn with rage.

"I wanted to save our family," he snarled, twisting his arm out of her grip. Yuharu's talons tightened to avoid slipping off his shoulder. "I wanted to *do* something. For Ojiisan—for us!"

"He wanted to help," Yuharu said.

"*No,*" Mama spat. There was venom in her voice. It pierced Kohei's skin. It *stung.* "If he wanted to help, he

would have stayed. He would never have run off by himself and—and nearly *drowned!* And left me all alone to pick
up the pieces! If he wanted to help—"

"But I didn't drown!" Kohei insisted. "I swam down
to the palace, and I got answers—answers you never gave
me! I met Ryuuji, and Ojiisan's ryū, and they told me
everything."

Recognition flickered in Mama's eyes. "Ryuuji," she
said.

"Yes, and—"

"What did he give you?" she asked, accusingly.

Kohei blinked. "What?"

Mama bared her teeth. "I remember Ryuuji," she said.
"I remember all those grand, ancient monsters. They gave
gifts like they were free—they gave your father knowledge, and—and *hope*—but gifts aren't free! Hope is not
free. And when it was all over, they left, went and *hid* in
the ocean, left the rest of us to clean up their *mess*, and
when Denjirō—"

Mama's voice cracked, and she clamped her mouth
shut.

Kohei felt like his whole body was about to crack.
He'd heard Mama say Papa's name a few times in his life,
in quiet moments, those odd times when they found some
peace, when everything felt still and somber and the air
was just a little bit cold. But she had never spoken of him

loudly. She always whispered of him—like he was a secret that only a few people were lucky enough to know.

The air was not cool or somber anymore.

Everything was burning.

Mama's face twisted, and for a fraction of a second, Kohei thought she might actually, physically catch fire. But then she pushed herself back down into some distant, hidden place; her expression settled and she released Kohei. She smoothed out his hair and straightened his collar.

The pain hadn't gone away. It was inside her and it could not be stopped, because she would not let herself burn. Just like Ojiisan, she would not let herself heal. There was nothing left of the young, impulsive, passionate girl that Mukashi remembered.

Mama looked down at Kohei, and she was as blank and numb as the snowy statues of Old Ryūgū-jō. "Your grandfather is resting at home," she said. "He was scared for you. He wanted to go out and search for you, but he was too weak, and it made him angry."

She turned on her heel and stalked away. Yuharu draped her tail over the back of Kohei's neck, the same way she always did when he had nightmares as a baby.

"It's okay," she murmured. "I think we'll ride home with the Carters."

14

Forgive Means Forget

*K*ohei *tucked himself* in the Carters' back seat and tried to convince himself he didn't exist. Isolde was there too, but she seemed scared to say anything about what had happened. Between their seats, Cheshire and Yuharu guarded the precious ōyatama—every time the car tires hit a bump in the pavement, they braced it with their claws, not wanting it to fall.

To Kohei, it just looked like a rock. A lumpy, ugly rock.

Everything was silent. When Kohei looked out the window, he could see life as usual moving past, but it felt like he was watching a film; it wasn't *real* life. The things he saw—people walking to the market, families bickering, messengers on bicycles—existed, but they were distant and unreachable, like legends. Like cowboys and big ryū.

"Isolde," he said quietly. "Do you ever wish you weren't born after a war?"

Isolde frowned at him. "What?" she said.

Kohei shrugged one shoulder.

Outside the car window, a man said something in his wife's ear, and she burst out laughing, punching his arm playfully.

"It's just—I see my grandfather and my mother, and I think about all the horrible things they've been through!" Kohei burst out. He saw Isolde's parents stiffen in the front seat, but he didn't care if they heard, not now. "And I realize how easy my life is, and I just think—*wow, he must hate me so much*. He must hate how stupid and tiny all my problems are. He wakes up from his nightmares, and he's so alone and so angry, and I can't do anything about it—I can't even share his sadness. There's nothing I can do. He must think I'm so *silly*." Kohei glanced at Isolde. "Everyone who's lived through a war is like that, I think—so *alone*. And I know it's awful, but I wish I could be alone with them. I wish I was hurting too badly to think, because at least then I would be with my family." He turned to her, pleading. "Does that make sense?"

Isolde didn't look at him, and she didn't answer for a long time.

"It does," she said, finally, softly. "It definitely does. Sometimes, I feel like every person I know is fighting their own personal war, and I can't fight with them. That was one reason why . . ." She tipped her chin at the egg that Cheshire and Yuharu were guarding in silence. "My problems aren't the same as yours, and yours aren't the same as mine. And Cheshire has his own nightmares, and my parents . . ." She lowered her voice, glancing at her mom and dad. They were pretending not to listen, but Isolde wasn't fooled. She continued in a whisper so low, even Kohei could barely hear her. "Mom is Japanese-American. Dad is Jewish. And they've been through so much, so many things that make *my* life look like *nothing*, but also—well, I have parts of them. And sometimes I think they don't have enough of me."

"And Naomi would have been different," Kohei whispered back.

Isolde gave him a sharp look. "She *is* different."

Kohei took a deep breath. *Ganbatte, ne. Perseverance.*

He stuck out his hand. "I promise to be your ally," he said, clearly enough for everyone in the car to hear. "I promise to take your battles seriously. Even if they're different from mine. I promise I'll be there, by your side." He swallowed. "Deal?"

Isolde studied his face, her mouth curving into the beginnings of a smile.

"Deal," she said.

She took his hand, squeezed it, and pulled him into the tightest hug ever.

Ojiisan was asleep at home, like Mama had said. As soon as Kohei stepped into the bedroom doorway, he knew for sure that his grandfather should not have left the hospital. His eyes were closed and his breathing was shallow. He was pale. He was almost gone. He should have stayed where the doctors could look after him.

But Kohei had run. Kohei had left.

And Ojiisan had wanted to run after him.

The room was so quiet. Mama had left the window open when she left for the station, and the dark orange of early sunset flooded every corner of the room, illuminating the thin layer of dust that had accumulated *everywhere*.

Mama was nowhere to be seen. But her voice echoed through the walls of their cardboard-box apartment. *Ayamarinasai*, it insisted. *You will apologize.*

You will apologize, because this is all your fault.

Isolde's parents, exhausted by the events of the past couple days, went directly to their own apartment downstairs. Isolde stayed with Kohei, just as she'd promised. She hung back near the doorway, clutching the unhatched dragon egg. As Kohei shuffled toward Ojiisan's bed, he felt

Yuharu's weight slip from his shoulder and heard the patter of tiny claws against the floor as she scampered to join Isolde and Cheshire by the door.

It wasn't that she was deserting him. She was giving him privacy.

If Isolde was correct—and she often was, whether Kohei wanted to admit it or not—today would be the day Kohei heard Ojiisan's stories for the first and last time.

He lowered himself into the basket seat at Ojiisan's side. He didn't want to look at the old man; the sight of his grandfather's face, pale and drawn, made his stomach clench like he was about to throw up. But he had to look, didn't he? He *had* to.

He was exhausted, like Ojiisan. He was finished, like Ojiisan. But . . .

"Tadaima," he whispered.

I'm home.

Ojiisan's eyes flickered open, and the sight of his gaze— crystal-clear, shrewd shards of obsidian—made Kohei's heart catch. When was the last time he'd seen Ojiisan's eyes unclouded?

Ojiisan seemed to recognize Kohei's astonishment.

The corner of his mouth twitched. "It's a funny thing," he said. "There was no beer in the hospital gift shop."

Kohei let out a sound that was either a sob or a laugh—he wasn't sure which. "The hospital has a *store?*" he said.

Ojiisan closed his eyes and sank back into his pillows.

Kohei cleared his throat. "Sir," he said. "I would like to—to . . ."

To what? Apologize? That seemed unfair. How was this Kohei's fault? It was his father who'd left, and his grandfather who drank, and his mother who swept everything broken under their living room rug. All Kohei had done was try to fix things—why was no one else apologizing? Why did he have to—

"Gomenasai," Kohei murmured, bowing his head. And as the apology left his lips, a calm coolness washed over him like sea-foam—some deep part of him relaxed, and the weight on his shoulders dissolved. "I am sorry. I hurt you even though I didn't mean to. I am sorry for that."

Ojiisan didn't move.

"Ki ni shinai de," he said gruffly. *Don't worry about it.* "Daijōbu."

And, unlike Mama, he actually meant it.

Kohei let out a long, slow breath, and Ojiisan turned his head against his pillow to study Kohei's face. "You came back," he said. "Why?"

"Why wouldn't I?"

Ojiisan shrugged. "I haven't given you many reasons to call this place home," he said. His gaze flickered around the room, up at the half-painted ceiling. "I would not have come back."

"I never meant to leave forever. I just—" Kohei broke off, remembering what Mukashi had said.

This was the man who had reported Papa to the government, who had him sent into exile. Whose daughter—Mama—left home because of it.

And Mama never *really* came back, did she?

Kohei blinked a few times, choking. *Ki ni shinai de,* his grandfather had said. He'd offered forgiveness, and Kohei had taken it. But Kohei wasn't the only one who needed to apologize, was he?

All he'd *ever* done was try to fix something that was already broken. Shouldn't he get an apology in return? Why did grown-ups *never* acknowledge their own mistakes, when those were usually the mistakes that mattered most?

Heat rose in Kohei's cheeks. The reasonable part of his brain looked around warily, wondering if it was time to bolt. Would it be wrong to yell at a man on his deathbed?

Sure, that voice of reason said. *But it would be wrong to forgive him too.*

Usually, Kohei's reasonable side was just a sarcastic, slightly more logical version of himself. But this time, other voices echoed along with it: Mukashi, Isolde, Yuharu.

And Papa.

So Kohei did not yell.

But he did not forgive either.

"I met him, Ojiisan," he said, very quietly. *Gaman, Kohei. Endure.* "I went to Ryūgū-jō, and I met your ryū."

Ojiisan's face was inscrutable.

"He never told me his name. He told me to call him Mukashi, but I never convinced him to tell me what he was actually called . . ."

"*Genji.*"

"Genji." Kohei frowned. "He told me many things. He—he misses you, you know."

"Does he," said Ojiisan, so quietly that Kohei almost didn't hear him. "Well. There will never be another ryū quite like him, will there?"

"I hope not," said Kohei.

There was a long pause.

The floor creaked behind them—the sound of Isolde's footsteps as she edged tentatively forward. "Kohei?" she said.

Kohei turned, startled, to see her holding the unhatched dragon egg out to him. She smiled at him, uncertain,

then looked to Ojiisan. "Sir," she said. "Have you ever hatched a dragon egg before?"

Ojiisan was too weak to get out of bed, so Kohei and Isolde built a makeshift nest of spare blankets while Yuharu and Cheshire prepared their scales. The ōyatama looked so small, swathed in decades-old linen on the bedside table. Ojiisan tilted his head to look at it. "That's a rock," he said.

"A super-earthly rock," Kohei corrected him.

Yuharu gave both of them a dirty look. "*It*," she said, "has seen more of Earth's history than all living humans put together. It's a very *good* rock. Its personality is unique."

"Is it friendly?" Isolde asked.

"Very friendly. Like an excited puppy or a babbling river. It can't wait to be alive." Yuharu glanced pointedly at Ojiisan.

"Mmph," Ojiisan said. "Get on with it, then."

Yuharu clambered over Kohei's shoulder to press her scale into the ōyatama's outer crust.

Isolde's breath hitched as the core of the igneous rock began to glow. Kohei knew without asking that she was thinking of Naomi. But Yuharu was right—this ōyatama was different from the last. It had its own personal character, its own energy. It didn't pulse with warmth, it *surged*,

like an icy wave, lapping and giggling like a snowstorm chasing its own tail. Kohei glanced at Ojiisan, wondering if, perhaps . . .

No. There was no sign of emotion in the old man's expression. The deep lines of his face were as still as death.

Kohei looked away. "Cheshire?" he croaked.

Isolde held Cheshire out in both hands so that he could reach the nightstand.

The ōyatama quieted at Cheshire's gentle touch, almost like it was contemplating something—not in a sad, withdrawn way, but a wondering way, like it had realized it was holding something unspeakably precious close to its heart.

"Is it okay?" Ojiisan asked.

Daijōbu?

Kohei nodded. "It's becoming something," he explained. "That's all."

The ōyatama shuddered. It *giggled*.

And the shell cracked.

She wasn't at all like Naomi, in a lot of ways. There was a different shine to her scales, a darker sort of glimmer. But she had the same strong legs, the same tufts of silky fur, and those same, lovely eyes—violet, with big, dark centers.

She was a million other things too. She was a million stories that hadn't happened yet. Kohei saw them overlapping, flashing by in her every movement: Isolde speaking Japanese in college . . . Kohei visiting New York . . . Ojiisan's funeral . . .

Oh, goodness. *Ojiisan.*

There was a long stretch of near-silence as the new mixed dragon peered around at the world for the first time. Yuharu went to greet her right away, and Cheshire and Isolde soon followed, but Kohei could only sit there, frozen. This new dragon was beautiful, lovely enough to make Kohei scared—not for himself, but for Ojiisan. He wasn't sure which would be worse: if his grandfather was angry, or if he still felt nothing.

Kohei wasn't sure if he'd ever be able to look up.

He took a breath. He counted to thirty.

He looked up.

Ojiisan had tears running down his cheeks. *Tears.* Kohei had never seen a grown man cry, never mind his grandfather.

Crying? *Ojiisan?*

Maybe he was weeping with rage. That was a logical explanation, wasn't it? Or perhaps he was weeping with sadness, because this was too strange, or—or maybe those

weren't actually tears. Maybe Kohei was seeing things. He was tricking himself.

Kohei looked at his grandfather's eyes. No, those *were* tears. And it didn't matter if they were sad tears or angry tears, because even the worst feelings meant that better feelings were possible. Crying meant that, someday, the crying would stop.

Kohei let out a shaky breath. Finally, he felt like he could breathe.

Ojiisan extended one finger to the new mixed dragon. He was hesitant, but she wasn't—she pressed the pads of her paws against his skin and looked up at him adoringly. She blinked her deep, dark eyes at him and wagged her tail.

Ojiisan let out a sound that was close to a laugh but was more likely a sob—a *real* sob. "Oh, Kohei," he said, wiping his eyes with his other hand. "Oh, my boy. What have you done?"

It was not an accusation. It was a thank-you.

15
The Untold Tales of Arahata Kohei

Friday evenings were magical even under normal circumstances, but now, according to Isolde, they were even better than actual weekends.

Because Friday evenings were when the Carter and Fujiwara families drove to the hills by the sea, blankets and picnic baskets in tow, to let their little dragons frolic in the tall grasses. Cheshire, the eldest and most austere, preferred to settle in a high place and keep a watchful eye on those he loved. Yuharu and baby Chōko—Ojiisan's new mixed ryū-dragon—were happy to roll around in the grass, pouncing on each other and play-fighting like puppies. Chōko was a healthy, normal-sized little dragon, but she was still bigger than Yuharu, and the older dragons

were out of practice. More often than not, Chōko emerged from their scuffles victorious.

Ojiisan looked so proud of her. He wasn't allowed to play with the dragons, or walk long distances, or even leave the house more than once per week. He'd been back to the hospital a few times, especially when the spring weather got unseasonably cold. Their apartment was relatively new, but it still didn't have electric heat, and the warmth of a kotatsu heater wasn't enough for someone with a chill so deep in their bones.

Still, Ojiisan was content to sit with Cheshire, watching the world in silence and occasionally shooting a concerned glance at Mama, who always sat on the sidelines too, apart from everyone, with her lips pressed tightly together.

Kohei heard her crying sometimes. It was like when he was little, and he'd find her weeping in the kitchen. Back then, he'd felt so sorry for her. He could remember how awful it felt to not know how to help her. But things were different now—Kohei wasn't sure if he should pity her at all.

Because pity was simple, and the world was so much more complicated now. Mama wanted to take back the years she'd lost, but Kohei wanted so badly to grab her and drag her into the present. Wasn't she losing *these* years now too? These were *his* years, and she was throwing them away!

Still. At least they had Friday evenings. These were those rare hours that seemed to exist in a different world from the rest of the week—in the dimness of dusk, the whirring of a hundred cicadas. The breeze was cool and warm at the same time, and it made the tall grass seem softer somehow.

Kohei and Isolde sat together on Friday evenings. That's what friends were for. They didn't speak a lot, because friends weren't always for speaking. Kohei was happy enough to know she was there. Usually, after school, they spent some time in the alleys around their apartment building, sitting on wooden crates abandoned by harried street food vendors and listening to the sounds of the city at work. On difficult days, Isolde would get up and pace back and forth, muttering about everything that bothered her. When that happened, Kohei got up too, hopping over the sewer grates in a sort of dance. He'd listen, but not say much.

Lots of days were hard. But this was a Friday evening, and Friday evenings meant peace.

Isolde was humming to herself, too quietly for Kohei to identify the song. Things had gotten better for her since the start of the school year—she even had a new friend, Isamu, a genius kid who'd skipped two grades and was too shy to talk to anyone else.

Sure, Isolde *seemed* happy. But Kohei knew better than to take that for granted. His mother had looked happy for twenty years—well, sort of—and now, she was all torn to pieces, and she never talked, not even to say, *Daijōbu*.

Kohei hadn't realized, before his trip to Ryūgū-jō, that he could go his entire life without knowing what the people around him truly felt. Particularly when they'd managed to convince themselves that they didn't know either.

Mama did know. Maybe that was the problem.

That day—that lovely, soft, dim Friday evening—Kohei felt Mama lower herself into the grass at his side. "Did he tell you?" she asked quietly.

Kohei's heart thumped; he exchanged a look with Isolde, whose eyes had gone all wide.

"Who do you mean?" Kohei asked.

"Ryuuji," Mama said. "And whoever else was down there."

Isolde gulped, shifting away like a mouse who'd woken up next to a cat. Kohei was grateful—this seemed like it should be a private conversation. But he also kind of wished she would stay, just in case Mama . . . exploded, or something.

"Um." Kohei looked down at his fingers, which were clasped in his lap and smudged with dusty dirt. "They told me a lot of things. Mostly about Ojiisan."

"And your father? That we were exiled?"

Kohei lifted one shoulder. "Sort of. Not all of it. But I met Ojiisan's ryū, and he . . . well, he told me some stories."

"Mm."

There was a long pause.

Mama chuckled. It was an actual laugh, which Kohei had never heard from her before. It wasn't pleasant or amused; it was more like the kind of sound Isolde made when Kohei did something strange.

A young and impulsive laugh, maybe.

"When you ran away," Mama said, "I was angry."

"I know," said Kohei. "I remember."

"I thought—" She hesitated. "I thought I was angry because you'd acted so much like your father, and being like your father is—well, it's always a bit dangerous. Now, I think it was something else . . .

"I think I was scared because you acted so much like me."

Kohei had no idea what to say, so he kept studying his hands like they were the most interesting things in the world.

Mama shook her head. A lock of graying hair fell over her eyes. "Your grandfather likes to think of your father as the wild radical who stole me away," she muttered, swiping at it irritably. "That's why he insisted you take his name once Denjirō was gone. He saw your father as a bringer of chaos—like the Arahata name itself was a curse. But he didn't understand." She turned to look at Kohei. "My husband thought with his mind, not his heart. He taught me how he looked at the world, but I . . . *I* was the one who convinced him to take risks. *Me.*"

She hesitated. "Did anyone at Ryūgū-jō tell you how he died?"

Kohei nodded, numb.

Mama made a low, bitter noise. "Well," she said. "Now you know. He dove into the sea in the middle of a typhoon. To protect us, maybe. But it was *reckless*. If I convinced him to do it, I promise I didn't mean to. All I know is that it wasn't like him to act so impulsively. It was strange." She nudged Kohei to make him look at her; her eyes were so serious. "All your life, I've tried to raise you to be safe—to act like your father did before I met him, before I changed him. But still, you were drawn to the ocean, to the ryū. I failed."

Kohei shook his head. "You didn't," he said. "You didn't . . ."

He felt like he was sitting on the edge of a rocky cliff, not a quiet, grassy spot in the Japanese countryside. One wrong move, and it would crumble, and they'd both fall.

"*No,*" he said firmly. "I don't remember much about Papa, but I remember how I felt when I was with him. I think maybe he loved me." He raised an eyebrow at

Mama, and saw her nod. "So I think—I think *I'm* the one who changed him. Because if he thought that the ryū were coming up from Ryūgū-jō, and that they might cause another war, he would've done anything in the world to stop it, even if it was impulsive and risky. Because he knew I wouldn't survive something like that, and he would've felt responsible if he didn't stop it. He would've thought—"

Kohei's words suddenly stopped coming; they choked him so he could barely breathe. But he must've said enough, because—for the first time in a very long time—Mama smiled.

An actual smile.

It wasn't the kind of smile that touched her mouth, but Kohei could see it in her eyes. "He did love you," she said. "He loved you more than anything in the world. And you're still so much like him."

There was a long pause.

"He cherished the future he dreamed for you," Mama murmured. "He came up with new stories, every night, of the things you might do when you were grown. That's what hope is, I think: remembering that there are stories we haven't told yet. We'll have to come up with some new ones for him, won't we? Together."

Kohei smiled. It was an actual smile too—the kind that came with a future.

They had *plenty* of stories to tell.

AUTHOR'S NOTE

There are lots of ways to translate a Japanese sentence, and lots of ways to transliterate one too. That's why, when people write Japanese words using English letters, you'll sometimes see doubled vowels (like in *kawaii*), or extra vowels (like in *arigatou*). For the most part, I use diacritical marks, like the line over the letter *u* in *ryū*. The Chinese pinyin system uses a lot of symbols like these (e.g., "dynastic lóng families"), but the Japanese versions are much simpler—instead of representing a particular tone, the line mark just indicates that a vowel is "longer," or more emphasized, than the others.

So, *ryū* is pretty simple to pronounce! The letter *r* is almost rolled, but not as strongly as it would be in Russian or Spanish; all you have to do is put the tip of your tongue against your front teeth when you say it. The letter *y* is pronounced like the "y" sound in *youth*, and *ū* is pronounced "oo." To say, "I really like dragons," as I'm sure you do, you'd say, "Ryū ga daisuki." Go ahead, give it a try! I'll be sure to pass the message along to Yuharu.

There are two titles in this novel that don't have diacritics: Ojiisan and Ryuuji. I decided to Romanize them differently as a substitute for honorifics, which are special sentence structures and words in Japanese that are used to

show extra respect. *Ojīsan* is a respectful way of saying *grandfather*, while the humbler version of the word, which Kohei would use to talk *about* his grandfather to people outside their family, is *sofu*. There's no good way to translate honorifics into English, but I thought that certain words and names should *look* different from the others, even in a subtle way.

I called my own grandfather *Ojiisan*, and my grandmother *Obaasan*. They had lots of stories that I'll never get to hear, from accounts of wartime exile to the names of long-lost siblings. This book is written in their honor.

ACKNOWLEDGMENTS

This story would not be remotely book-shaped if not for the kindness and patience of the people who, for reasons I still don't fully understand, saw the earliest versions of the manuscript and thought: "Yeah, this could be something cool someday." As such, thank you to my agent, Mary C. Moore, for her advocacy; to my editor, Meghan Maria McCullough, for her compassion, vision, and wit. Thank you to Diana Babineau, copyeditor-extraordinaire, and to Tatsuro Kiuchi for his astonishing cover art. Endless, immeasurable gratitude to the whole team (marketing, publicity, design, *everything*) at Levine Querido.

I have several additional thank-yous to give to Van Hoang, Zoe Hana Mikuta, and Amber-Rose Reed, my brilliant beta readers. Many hugs to my father, who read a novella I wrote in the eighth grade and marked several *very* specific passages that made him cry, and my mother, who—upon hearing that her seven-year-old daughter wanted to be an author when she grew up—said, "Wonderful! You can do that *now.*"

I learned to write books while pretending to take notes in most, if not all, of my classes. For that reason and more, I am forever indebted to the academic communities at

Amos A. Lawrence Elementary School and Brandeis University, and to the countless teachers who've shaped my life for the better: Catherine Mannering, Jan Yourist, and Christopher M. Freeman, to name just a few.

Special thanks to everyone I met at Columbia University's Summer Program for High School Students (except Zoe, who already got a shoutout as a beta reader—limit one per person!). Equally special thanks to my classmates in Professor Plotz's worldbuilding class (ENG 38a), whose hot takes on Tolkien will forever be a part of my soul.

And lastly but certainly not least-ly: to the family I've known only briefly, to those I'll never meet, and to those who have been here all along. Thank you, thank you, thank you.